Who Do You Love?

By Leon Rooke

Novels

Fat Woman
Shakespeare's Dog
A Good Baby

Short Story Collections

Last One Home Sleeps in the Yellow Bed
Vault
The Love Parlour
The Broad Back of the Angel
Cry Evil
The Magician in Love
Death Suite
The Birth Control King of the Upper Volta
Sing Me No Love Songs I'll Say You No Prayers
A Bolt of White Cloth
How I Saved the Province
The Happiness of Others

Drama

Sword/Play
Krokodile
Ms. America
A Good Baby

Editor (with John Metcalf)

Best Canadian Stories, 81
Best Canadian Stories, 82
The New Press Anthology #1
The New Press Anthology #2
The Macmillan Anthology #1
The Macmillan Anthology #2

Who Do You Love?

stories by

Leon Rooke

M&S

Canadian Cataloguing in Publication Data

Rooke, Leon
  Who do you love?

ISBN 0–7710–7713–0

I. Title.

PS8585.065W5 1992   C813'.54   C92–093469–2
PR9199.3.R66W5 1992   74809

Design by Randolph Rozema

Printed and bound in Canada on acid-free paper

McClelland & Stewart Inc.
The Canadian Publishers
481 University Avenue
Toronto, Ontario M5G 2E9

For Jonathan

Acknowledgments

Many of these stories appeared previously in U.S. and Canadian magazines and anthologies, often under different titles. Many of these stories appear here in revised form. The author is grateful to the editors of the following:

The Quarterly for "Shut Up," "Drivers," and "I Want To Know the Answer."

Grand Street for "The Willies," "Light Bulbs," and an earlier version of "Typical Day in a Desirable Woman's Life."

TriQuarterly, Pushcart Prize Stories 1987, Best Canadian Stories 1987, and *Fiction of the Eighties: A Decade of Stories From TriQuarterly* for "Who Do You Love?" (published as "Blue Baby").

TriQuarterly and *Harper's* for "Pretty Pictures."

The Chatahoochie Review for "Mama Tuddi Tried" (published as "Mama Tuddi").

Mississippi Review for "Sweethearts" and an earlier version of "Blues Roots or You Tear Me Apart" (published as "Blues Roots").

Prairie Fire for another version of "Sweethearts."

Exile for "Daddy Stump" and an earlier version of "LR Loves GL."

Waves for "Neighborhood Watch."

Descant for "Regeneration" and "The People in the Trees" (published as "Turnpike").

Border Crossings and *The Macmillan Anthology 3* for "Admiral of the Fleet."

Review: Latin American Literature and Arts for "Cornfields."

New: West Coast Fiction for an earlier version of "Art" (published as "Paintings, Watercolors, Hand-Painted Flowers").

Now Magazine for an earlier version of "The Bucket Brigade" (published as "The Bucket").

The American Voice for an earlier version of "Lunch Detail" (published as "Water Over the Bridge").

Quarry for "Choirmaster's Report."

Carousel for an earlier version of "Mate's Rap" (published as "Wife Talk").

*   *   *

The author is grateful to the Canada Council, the Ontario Arts Council, and the University of Western Ontario/ Canada Council Artist-in-Residence Program, for value received during the writing of this book.

Contents

Who Do You Love?

Who Do You Love?

There was a time down in North Carolina when nothing ever happened.

There was the time up north in the Yukon when a man I knew locked up another man I knew inside a freezer and the man froze.

There were those times and there were other times.

I don't know which times to tell you about.

There was the time when I was twelve and riding a bicycle around and around a small shrub in the backyard and the front tire hit a brick and the bicycle crumpled beneath me and I broke a tooth and she did not care.

I am convinced she did not care.

So there was that time too.

There were the times she would bounce me on her knees and ask, Who do you love most, him or me? You didn't remember him or anything about him, but there were those times she asked that. He was like your nickel which rolled between the floorboards into the utter, unreachable darkness of the world. He was like that. Who do you love most, him or me? And though you knew the answer you never said a word, not one. You would only hang your head and wait for the knee-ride to begin again. She would stop the ride to take your face in her hands and ask that. And though you knew the answer, knew it to the innermost ache of your heart, you never said a word, not one.

You couldn't say, Ride me, Mama. You could only squint at the thin darkness between the floorboards and wonder what else over the long years had fallen between those cracks.

Him or me?

For years and years she asked this and you always knew but never answered, and now you are here by her bedside and still you can't.

So there were those times. Some of the times were good times, but they do not belong here. I don't know where they belong.

Here is another one. Sometimes on a dark night you could stand under a tree in front of your house and see two naked fat people in the upstairs room in the house across the street.

I thought, If only they knew how ugly they are.

I thought, Why do they do that?

I thought, Why don't they turn off that light?

The fat man up there lived in another place, lived across the river, and I thought he should stay in the place he came from.

My friends on that street would gather under that tree and they would say, Oh baby, look at them go, and you never could get your friends away from that tree. Shut up, they would say, what's eating you?

My mother was a friend of this woman. She was to be seen in this woman's company, in this fat woman's company, she was to be seen with them. I wondered whether my mother knew what went on up there with this fat couple, and why, when she went out on double dates, she had to go out with people like this.

He had a car, that's why.

On Saturday nights they went to dances together in a place called Edgewater, Virginia.

I stand corrected on this one small matter: I said "car" but it was not a car. His was a stingy little truck, dusty and black, with narrow, balding tires and corncobs and empty fertilizer sacks in the rear. When they went out to these dances the fat woman would sit up under the fat man's arms and my mother would sit in the cab on her date's lap, her head folded up against the ceiling, and all four would be hooting with laughter.

That was one time.

There was that time I broke a tooth falling against a brick while riding my bicycle around and around this little shrub and my mother said, Now no girl will ever marry you, but I knew she didn't care. She hardly even looked, scarcely even glanced at me, because I wasn't bleeding.

I got hit in the jaw once with a baseball, there was that time.

I pulled long worms out of my behind, there were those times, and I didn't tell her.

There was the time a dentist, my first dentist, took out an aching tooth, the wrong tooth, with a pair of garage pliers and charged two dollars.

You could see those worms up in white circles on my cheeks and across my shoulders and people would look at you, they'd say, Look at that boy, he has worms.

You took a folded note to the store one time which you were not supposed to read, but you read it and it said, Give him head lice powder, I will pay you later.

You stole a nickel from her purse one time and it rolled between the floorboards and you have not yet confessed that.

You were such a nice little boy, so sweet and good.

You had to sit on a board when you got a haircut. You'd

3

see the barber pick up the board and sling it up over the arms of the chair and you wanted to hit him.

You put a penny in the weight machine in front of the drugstore and got your fortune told. You would put in the penny or one of your friends would, and then that friend would step up on the scale with you or you would step up beside him, step up carefully, not to jiggle or the red cover would slam down over the numbers, and then one of you would step off, step carefully off, not to jiggle, and the numbers would roll back to reveal your own true weight, although both of you had the same fortune.

For two years I never weighed more or less than eighty-seven pounds. There was that time.

Women – young girls, ladies – would come to the door and they would ask, Is So-and-So here? Where is So-and-So? But you weren't supposed to tell them, even if you knew, because So-and-So had washed his hands of these women, was done with them, yet they wouldn't leave him alone.

Policemen knocked on the door, too, they too wanted to know where So-and-So was.

So-and-So was in trouble with women, with the law, with the family and with everyone else, and what you heard was he was no good, he was mean, he cared about no one, he would as soon hit you as look at you, but he was my mother's brother and she was ever defending him and hiding him and if anyone didn't like it they could go climb a pole.

You had to go to the store to buy your mother's Kotex, because no one else would or no one else was around, and that was terrible. The storekeeper would say, Speak up, boy, and you would again grumble the word. He would put the Kotex up on the counter and everyone would stare at it, would say this or that, they'd look at me, look me over closely, then the storekeeper would wrap the box in brown paper like a slab of meat and take your money and go away rubbing it between his fingers.

Sometimes a strange dog would come up and follow you for a bit, follow you home even, even stand scratching at the door, but you never knew whose dog it was or what name you could call it except Dog or what means you could devise to make it stay.

Mrs. Whitfield next door refused to return any hit ball that landed in her yard.

The one pecan tree in this place I am talking about was surrounded by a high fence and you could not reach the limbs even with poles and no matter how hard or long you tried.

At night you threw rocks at the light hanging over the gravel street and when you hit it you ran fast as you could, because Mrs. Whitfield would be calling the law.

The policemen patrolled these streets like beings from another side of the world.

A boy my age jumped or fell from the water tower at the edge of town, there was that time.

There was the time a car was parked in the same alley that ran behind our house, with a hose hooked up from the exhaust to a window, but only the woman died. The man with her had awakened in the night, had changed his mind and fled. She was some other man's wife and her blouse was open and below the waist she had nothing on except her green shoes. My mother said to us all, she said, What kind of scum would leave her like that?

The town smelled. It smelled because of the paper mills and sometimes a black haze would cover the sky and you would have to hold your nose.

Those fat, naked people in the room upstairs, you would see them drink from a bottle sometimes. You would see

5

them with their arms around each other and then a hand would reach down to the windowsill and pick up the bottle.

You would see the light bulb hanging from their ceiling and a fly strip dangling to catch the flies.

A body was discovered one summer in a stream called the Dye Ditch, the stream you had to cross to reach grammar school, but you went down to look at that place in the ditch where the body was discovered but no one was there, no corpse was there, and after a while you didn't hear anyone speak of it and you never knew who it was had been stabbed in that ditch. The ditch was deep, with steep clay walls, the walls always wet, wet and smooth and perfect, but clay was not a thing you knew to do anything with. You found a shoe in the woods just up from the bank, a shoe with the tongue missing, and you said, This was the stabbed man's shoe and you asked yourself why So-and-So had done it, because of some woman, most likely.

Some days the ditch water was one color, some days another color, vile colors, and at other times it was a mix of many.

You couldn't dam up that stream although you spent endless days trying, and you put your bare foot in the stabbed man's shoes but you still didn't know why or how it had happened.

You were such a nice little boy. You were so nice. You tried making biscuits once as a surprise for your mother when she came in from work, but you forgot to mix lard in, and the salt and baking powder, and the biscuits didn't rise, and when she came in you'd forgotten to wipe up the flour from the table and floor.

She would sit you on her knees and hold your shoulders as she bounced you up and down and she would say, Which do you love best, him or me?

You were swinging on a tree-rope by the Dye Ditch, swinging high, into the limbs, and you let go and flew and when you landed a rusty nail came up all the way through your foot and as you hobbled the half-mile home you were amazed that it hurt so little and bled so little, and when you got home your brother pulled out the nail with pliers and your mother rubbed burning iodine over the wound and said, Be sure you wear clean socks for the next little while.

Three streets were paved, all others were gravel, and all of the streets were named after U.S. presidents. There was an uptown called Rosemary and a downtown called Downtown, and uptown was bigger, while Downtown was dying, was dead, but was the place you had to go through if you wanted for whatever reason to cross the river.

Across the river was nothing, it was death across the river. The fat man had come from across the river, so had my mother when she was fourteen and fleeing death, which was exactly how she spoke of it. Oh, honey, it was death on that farm.

He was down between the cracks, my father was, that's where he was.

There was another time, an early time, when I walked with my grandfather across the fields and when he stopped to pick up soil and crumble it and let it sift between his fingers I would pick up soil and do the same.

Your grandfather let you walk down the rows with him, he let you hold the plow, and he said, Just let the mule do the work, but you couldn't hold the plow handles and the reins at the same time and the plow blade kept riding up out of the ground. When you came to the end of a row the mule would stop and your grandfather would look at both of you, look and flap his hat against his leg, and say, Now let's see which of you has the better sense. You stood

7

behind your grandfather's chair in the evenings and combed his balding head, but your grandmother said, I've got enough plates to get to the table, why should I get theirs? Why can't she come and take away these that are hers and leave me with those that are mine?

No one asked her to marry that drinker.

Didn't we tell her sixteen was too young?

She made her own bed. There ain't one on their daddy's side ever had pot to pee in or knew what pot was for.

So there was the time she came and packed your goods, your brother and sister's goods, in a paper sack, and took you to town for the first time. The town was only seven miles away, but it was the first time and it was quite a town. It had a downtown called Downtown and an uptown called Rosemary, and she had two upstairs rooms downtown on Monroe Street, and you had to be very quiet up there because the woman who lived below lived alone and she was so stupid she thought every sound meant a thief was coming to steal her money.

She had a blue baby, this baby with an enormous blue head, and all of the light bulbs in her rooms were blue so that you wouldn't know she had a blue baby.

Every day for five days in the week, sometimes six, your mother left for work before daylight, you would hear the car out on the street honk for her, you would hear the car door slam, hear the engine, the roll of tires, and she would be gone. You would hear her moving softly about you, you would feel her tucking you in, then she would be gone. You went to school that first week and for five days stood in the woods watching the children at play outside, then the bell would ring and they would go inside, and when the yard had cleared you would tramp through the woods back home, you would dawdle at the Dye Ditch and check where you could and could not jump it and be amazed at all the vile colors, you would sit on the bank and grieve and tell yourself that tomorrow you would go inside with them. Then you would sneak up the stairs and never make a sound all day, just you and the blue baby and the baby's mother in that silent house. You would sit at the table drawing rings of water on the yellow top. At the end of the day your mother would come in with a bag of groceries, come in with a sweater looped over one arm, come in with cotton fuzz in her hair, and she would say, How do you like your new school, is it a nice school? How do you like your new friends?

She would sit you on her knees and bounce you and say, How is my handsome man today?

You were such a good little boy.

On Fridays you got up early to deliver the local paper and the people would not pay, they would say, it is not worth my nickel, and you kept returning but they rarely would pay, although they did not tell you to stop delivering their paper and if you did stop they would call the editor, they would say, Where's my paper?

There was the time I knocked on one door and my Uncle So-and-So answered without his clothes on and he said, You haven't seen me, you don't know where I am, and he gave me a dollar.

The blue baby died and went to heaven, but the woman downstairs did not change her light bulbs.

On Mondays you would take your mother's white blouse and black skirt to the cleaners and on Saturdays you would see her wearing these. You would see her in heels, her legs in nice stockings, her mouth red, and she would say, How do I look?

She would say, Say Hello to Monty, but you wouldn't.

She would say, He's so cute when he's pouting, and that would make you grin.

She would say, I'll be home early, but you stayed up late with your head pressed against the window and she never came, no, she never.

There was the time she said, You smell like four dead cats in a trunk, why don't you wash? And she flung your clothes off and scraped at your knees, elbows and heels, she twisted a cloth up in your ears, she said, This crust will never come off, and when she had your skin pink and burning she said, Your father is coming, you want to look nice for him, don't you?

But he didn't come, and I put back on my dirty clothes and hid under the house until past bedtime, until past the time she'd stopped walking the street and calling my name, and then I went in and would talk to no one.

There was the time she said, I want the three of you out of this house, I want you out this minute, if I don't get a minute's peace I will stab myself with these scissors. So she dressed you and your brother in identical *Little Boy Blue* short-pant suits with straps that came over the shoulder, and she washed your faces and necks and ears and slicked your hair down with water. She gave your sister thirty-six cents from her red purse and she said, Take them to see the moving picture show at the People's Theater and don't you dare come back until the picture is over. My sister said, Mama, how will we know when the picture is over? and my mother said, When the rest of the audience gets up to leave that's when you leave, and not a second before. So we trouped down to the movie, hurrying to get there because we couldn't imagine what it might be like to see a moving picture show. We entered in the dark and sat in seats at the very rear, while up on the screen you saw the back of a man's head and a woman with her head thrown back and they were kissing. We sat on the edge of our seats, holding hands, my sister in the middle and telling us not to kick our legs, as the man got into a jeep and drove off, not returning the wave of the woman who was running after him, and he got smaller and smaller in his jeep as the music got louder, and then we saw tears slide down the woman's face and she collapsed to her knees in the muddy road and in the next second the theater lights were rising and everyone was getting up. They were getting up, they were all leaving.

On the way home the three of us bawled and my sister said it wasn't worth thirty-six cents, it wasn't worth nothing and Mama must be crazy.

So that was that time and that is why I have hated movies to this day.

You weighed eighty-seven pounds for so many of those years.

You wore socks so stiff with filth you could barely work your feet into them in the morning. Your nose ran, always ran, and you wiped the snot on your sleeves until they turned stiff also, from cuff to elbow.

You would feel this tickling movement, this wriggling motion, while you sat on the toilet, and you'd stand up and wrench yourself over and there would be this long worm coming out of your behind. You couldn't believe it that first time, but here it was, proof that worms were living inside you, and it made you ache with the shame that if worms did, lived inside you, then what else could?

You will tell no one. You could be walking down the street and you'd feel it, feel the worm, and you'd reach a hand inside your britches and pull the worm all the way out and you'd think it never was going to stop coming.

Who do you love best, him or me?

There was the time all this ended, but you never knew when it was that time was, so it was as though that time never ended, which is one reason to think about it. I think about it because it ended, but never really ended, that is why I think about it.

They were always washing your ears.

They were always saying, Tie your shoelaces.

You were always being shoved one way or another by one person or another and you never gained an ounce through so many years.

We got home from the moving picture show fifteen minutes after we left and our mother was sitting in her slip in the kitchen chair, with her eyes closed and both wrists up white in her lap and her feet in a pan of water.

Cotton fluff was in her hair.

One year you asked your mother whatever happened to that fat old guy with the truck who went with that woman across the street, and she didn't know who you meant. Some days later, while washing her hair over a white bowl, she suddenly clapped her hands and said, Oh him, they are not going together any longer, it was never serious anyhow. It's just that he treated her decently and he wasn't a tightwad, and he liked good fun. Why are you asking about something like that?

Why are you? Sometimes I find myself thinking you are a strange little boy.

You're odd. That's how you strike me sometimes.

I think about it now because now she lies in this bed with tubes up her nose and tubes attached to her shaved head and she's holding my hand, or rather her hand is limp in mine and you can't hear her breathe. You can't see her chest rise and her lids never move. Her fingers are silent in mine.

You think of the man you knew who was locked up in the freezer in the Yukon and how he froze.

You think of the freezer and of opening the door, but when the door is opened after all of these years all you see is the freezer empty and the frosty tumble of air.

You think of these things and of those times.

She has been this way for an hour or more, not moving, and so have I, the two of us here, neither of us moving and nothing happening, her hand cold in mine and the night darkening and I still haven't answered.

Light Bulbs

The one thing I liked to do with my wife was confess. There were other things I liked doing with her too, but now is not the time for that. Stick around though. Who can tell?

What I liked confessing to with that woman were all the stupid, the impossible, the truly inconceivable or embarrassing secret acts I have been either party to or solely responsible for over the years. The sort of act that makes your face turn raw with shame and you want to head for oblivion's first corner. You're talking *priests*, your common clergy-type fellow, I wouldn't come within a mile of these with any of my tales. I'm talking *privacy*, that's what I mean. I'm talking the big horn up in the forehead that makes a fellow sleep with his hat on: that's the deal I mean.

Here is one I was a long time owning up to even with the wife. And why I told her was I knew she wouldn't laugh. Heart-on-the-sleeve. No, nothing was ever silly or funny or a matter of ridicule for the recent wife. You could surprise her, but not shake her. Pillar of salt. Anyway, here's the one. Bend an ear.

You know how in winter in this city, given our climate, the service station air pumps have their hoses removed. I'm talking *tires*, you understand, the big freeze. Your everyday automobile tires. And if your tires are like mine, and whose aren't, they go flat. One two three. You look down one day and there it is: I mean *flat*. So you got snow on the ground, ice in your lungs, your fingers frostbitten, and you go looking for the service station with true service. Miles and miles. And what you find is the little red box, but all the hoses removed. Maybe six in the whole city with the full equipment. Also as you hunt these working pumps you're thinking like time changes, like it marches on. I mean, there are a million things you see these days you can't even recognize. Men, women, dogs and cats, the items you see on display in a thousand stores. *What is it?* That's a reasonable question you ask yourself, our age and time.

So I can't find one. Not one air pump that can do its job. And my tire is wobbling on the rim, I'm chewing that rubber into dog meat. So finally I find one. I pull in and I'm filling my tire. Strangest air pump you ever saw. Funny red tank, lean and round, your twentieth-century model. Short hose. Nozzle won't fit. But I get it going. What's this? Dust? Is it sawdust? Well it's blowing anyway and it's freezing cold. Makes your fingers numb. Is that what they're putting into tires these days? Jesus, what was wrong with your simple air? That's what I'm thinking. But I'm getting the hang of it, I think I see some improvement in that tire.

So I'm hacking away at it when this other guy drives up to the self-service island. He goes about his business, filling his car, but I see him watching me. What the heck you doing? he asks me. And he won't let up. Jesus, is he ever staring. Finally he gets control of his emotions. He strolls near, but not too near. Like he doesn't want to take the *risk*, I mean. What are you doing? he asks. Okay, I don't mind talking to strangers. It won't kill me to be civil to the fellow, plus I'm imparting information. I'm putting air into this flat tire, I say. Uh-huh, he says, I thought so. And he watches me struggle with my tire another few minutes. But he's looking around as though wondering will he need any help. And I have the strongest sense that something is going wrong, and not only with my tire. What I sense is trouble. It's out there and I can feel it. So I try to hurry up the job. I've got this sawdusty stuff barooming out like snow over Missouri. These modern gadgets, I'm thinking, why can't they stick with the tried and the true? Then the guy makes up his mind and says: You think that's the air pump, do you? And me, I'm still being civil. I've got patience. I say, Well, it's got this red box, it's got a hose, though the nozzle isn't worth a fuck. And he says, You know what, buster? That's a fire extinguisher.

And he starts inside to pay.

Now you'd think this would mark the end of that episode. I'm an upstanding citizen, nice enough to your fellow man, as honest as the next guy. You, being me, wouldn't you go inside, confess to your deed, fork over fifty dollars to get that extinguisher refueled? Yes. Well yes. But I'll tell you, nothing could have induced me to take even one step that way. I ripped into my car and tore away.

Yes. Now it is precisely this brand of rare and remarkable ignorance that I would confess to. With my wife. Bar all others. It hurt. Oh the ache. But I had to have someone. I couldn't live with that fire extinguisher story imprisoned inside me.

Mind you, that's only an example.

Not your worst example by a long shot.

The wife sometimes didn't believe me. You've made that up. No one is that stupid, she'd say.

So I'd go on confessing. One item leading to another, as you know it will.

The times when I liked it best was when my confessions would get her own going. I can beat that, she'd say.

But she almost never could. I'd say I was the clear winner nine cases out of ten.

I mean, she was from another world altogether.

The time I fell down into that hole, she'd say. *Now that was stupid!*

And I'd have to laugh. Because the kind of hole she fell into, the troubles and silly episodes that happened to her, could have occurred with *anyone.*

Our sessions got right *mean* sometimes. They got stupid and mean, I mean, and eventually became a part of what we were talking about *in the first place.*

Can you see that?

It was not a lovely place to be. We were creating a history, that is to say, with which we *could not live.* Something had to give, one of us did, and the one giving first was me.

The truth. I confess it. I'm ashamed about it, but there you are.

No, that is not the end. There is more I must tell you and am I not here to get it off my chest? Absolutely.

Now I know where all this started. Where and when. When it started I was this little kid. So try seeing this part. We were snot-nose poor, in a land of the poor. That fact is crucial, and I can only unearth it, pull it out to be examined the way you would a spud on the table. Your big potato. Five dollars had to feed the family for a month, that was our kind of poor. But there was this one period when I had us spending nearly that much on light bulbs. Yes, light bulbs. Your ordinary – well, for the time and the place – household fixture. Your true poverty number. The kind you see these days in some old folks' home or in some dim, dusty, uninhabited *basement.*

There they'd be, hanging from twisty, swinging overhead cords. And I'd stroll by. Hey, what's *this?* I'd say. Is that a *light* bulb?

Your *bare* and *naked* light bulb I am talking about. In this town no one ever thought of shades. *Shades?* Are we being fancy? Are you kidding? Who can afford shades? You're talking *shade?* How would anyone see? You pay for light bulbs, you pay the electricity bill, you don't have a nickel left over, you're in debt for years to come, and you're talking *killing* half of what you've paid for? *Shading* that light? My God, are you crazy?

So shades hadn't been invented yet, that's what I'm saying.

Ugly? Why, yes, but they got the job done.

And there they'd be, hanging by their twisty, swinging cords, as I walked by. And what would I do? What was my dire sin? Is that what you're asking me?

I'd *swat* them. I'd swat them, knowing exactly what I was doing, for what they'd do when I swatted them was burn like Egypt for about one minute – one minute or two, everything bright as a carnival – and me over the huge expanse of that minute in a spellbound fit at the sheer *radiance*, the plain wonder, of that light. I'm talking *light*. Light like there must have been light at creation's first orbit, with the sun's first turning. Yes, by God, your *first* light.

Then they crackle and spit, those light bulbs would, and *very slowly* fade out. Sizzle out.

And I'm there in the darkness, you see, holding on to my light.

But what happens is my mother hears this spitting, sizzling shit and she starts running. She's in the kitchen, she starts running. She's outside chatting with neighbors, she starts running. Three blocks away even, she somehow knows and starts running. Damn you! she says. You little turd! Wait till I git my hands on you!

Oh *mama mia!* – that kind of mama.

But I'm long on my way by then. I've gone out in a

straight dive through the open or shut door. Do I want to stay and be killed? Don't be silly.

What I'd do is I would hang around dark alleys and hug your dark street corners and vow I'd never go home. Let Mama cool off. Let her go to the store and buy *another* light bulb. Wow, what an idea. I'd think of that minute of instant and glorious light, of how it turned the room into a mansion of near-blinding, beautiful white, and how that light shot out with such power and force that no walls could *contain* the son of a bitch. Do you finally know the kind of light I'm talking about?

Wouldn't you have?

So I'd go all through that and I'd rethink that fizzle too. That fizzle, the crackle and spit, the slow fade, and that beautiful second when I stood in the blackness with everything totally *stopped*.

Stopped, halted, backed up, come to its own black dead end.

Your universe-maker. Me. At dead center, in the black room, under the Virginia Electric and Power Company's pathetic swinging cord.

Oh VEPCO you know not what powers you have unleashed.

Then my mother running, as I've said. Shouting my name. *Little bastard, I'm going to kill you!*

Oh those thudding feet. That sound I loved as much as all the rest. And the pure wizardry with which I'd thumped those light bulbs. Never a miss. Never the need for a second attempt. Direct hit every time.

Sooner or later I'd go home and face the medicine. Of course I would. Under your usual circumstances was I not a normal, obedient, and home-loving child? Yes. And yes a second time. So my medicine then, and *harder on me than it is on you*, just as it's supposed to be.

But I tell you the medicine was never so tough I ever regretted my swatting or wasn't looking forward to the next time.

Not at that age anyhow. Not while I was a kid.

Because did it ever penetrate to me what that bulb cost? Was I a specialist in the economics of the marketplace? Are you kidding?

And this other little stab: *Would it have mattered?* Would I have mended my ways?

The *first* light: *oh you kid!*

So that's where it started. The confessional routines came later, after my marriage. Tell you the truth, that may be *why* I got married. Oh yes, I've suspicions about that. You want to know something else? I'm dying to tell you. Aside from this compatibility on the one crucial front, my wife wasn't remotely like me. No mutual interests, I am saying, not even one. *Not Even From The Beginning.* Doesn't that tell you something? Doesn't it speak a ton? And we knew it too. Honey, we can overcome those odds: that's what we said.

It gave us something else to confess to and mull over, right?

But our *age* difference: maybe in the final summation that was what defeated us. I'm talking years and years. Light-years. Jesus, sometimes I look back over our age difference and I wonder whether I was all there. Whether she was. The dogfights we had . . . well, you'd feel nothing but chagrin for the two of us.

Some of those sweettalks we had were A on the button, however. Don't get me wrong.

But, Christ, she's going to talk to me about dropping off into a *hole!* She's going to confess *that!* I mean, where *are* we? Are we talking on this earth – or some other place?

Who's the kid here: that's what I'm asking.

But funny I never got around to telling her about those light bulbs. Just couldn't enter into the heart of it somehow. Couldn't summon the . . . well, what might you call it? The majesty. That beauteous momentary illumination, the holiness . . . followed by that wondrous dark.

Or maybe I did tell her. Maybe she wasn't impressed or possibly saw it as something *not unlike* her holes.

Like to follow that up, ever I get a chance. Get an earful.

You haven't seen her have you?

You don't know where she is?

Here one day, the next day gone: that's all I know.

Wait, hold on. I think it's coming back to me: something she said, or did, or . . .

Nope, it's fled me now. I thought I had her there for a second.

But it was only my old mom, trying to sneak up on me.

The People in the Trees

I'll tell you something I never told anyone, the fat woman said.

We were all ears. We were all ears when the fat woman spoke. A minute ago it was an elephant sat on her. But we didn't believe that. She believed it, though, and the telling had some force. It's exactly how when a man is on top, she said, and you don't want any part of it. It's exactly like that. You wonder to yourself how it was he got up there. You wonder what it was you did. He's not up there because you're so beautiful, that's what you're thinking. It's what's going on in your mind, whether it's a man up there or an elephant.

"I know it's dumb, but that's how it felt when the elephant sat its big rear-end on me. He felt like about forty husbands all at once, and not one of them what you'd call a decent human being. That's how it felt."

I'd been wondering since that telling when an elephant would sit on me or a man would, and I'd been betting the elephant would get there first.

"You're not listening to me," she said. The fat woman said this to the whole room, and I couldn't deny it. "You're off dreaming," she said. "Probably thinking about sex and not thinking about what I'm saying one little bit. Life has changed, you know. It's changed so much I never know who I'm talking to. I don't know why I even try. Do you think even for a minute people in the olden days thought about sex with the frequency you do? Even for a minute? Hell no, they were too busy worrying would somebody hurl a spear into their chest or would the beans grow or their house fall down or how to beat the king's taxation and still keep their heads. But you, you think about it all the time, I know you do, I can tell by how your eyes glazed over when I mentioned that elephant sitting on me.

"Forget that elephant," she said.

She said we should all stand up and stretch our legs, and breathe through our noses for a bit.

None of us moved.

"Go to the window," she said, "and breathe some fresh air. There are times when I don't know what has got into people's brains. Did you just drive up to a pump? Did you say to the pumpperson, Well, just fill me up with twenty gallons of your regular?"

Still we didn't move. I yawned, but she didn't see it.

"You went to the wrong pump," she said.

"Why am I here?" she said. "Who brought me? Who is going to pay my fee? Are you wondering how I got into, or will get out of, this chair?"

I wasn't wondering about any of that. I wasn't wondering about anything.

I doubted anyone else was either. We were all such dead-beats. We hardly had a brain between us.

She apparently agreed. She said we all ought to be shot at sunrise.

She said she wished she'd never turned off the turnpike.

"Now I'm going to tell you about the time I was thin," she said. "But first somebody light me a cigarette. And, second, somebody take a look at their feet because I smell something on your shoes. All of you, you make me so mad. It's like you think I wrote some kind of management-ladder book and if you look at me long enough you're going to be up on the roof looking down at everybody else scrabbling in the dirt. Aren't you? I can tell you are by how your eyes are glazed over. I didn't write that book. What I'm here for is to show you how to discover how to have your emotions and deal with them, how to manage your interpersonal and negotiation skills and stop being a victim. That's what I'm here for but I don't like what I see and you've put me in a foul mood.

"Thank you," she said. "Thank you for the cigarette. What kind is it? I'll tell you this much. To find the secret of your life's end, your life's goals and plans, you got to see about controlling your non-verbal communication. None of you have control worth a shit. You got to think about what causes all those mixed signals and interior messages so coded you'd think they came from the moon. Maybe they do. So, first, figure out where they come from and what causes them and what goes into the code: then maybe you'll get somewhere. But I doubt it. You're a real lackluster bunch."

None of us replied to this. She was doing what everybody else did to us and we hadn't expected it.

She hadn't come cheap either.

"Now would somebody get me a bowl of ice cream and a bag of cookies, and I wouldn't frown on a Coke. I'm a big woman and it takes a lot to keep my sails high. I'm not saying anything else until the dish is down in front of me. You don't like it, then tough shit. For a nickel I'd be back on the turnpike and the lot of you could be here stewing in your juices. Now hop to it. You want a seminar, you want to know what your personal bill of rights are, then I'm here to tell you. I'm probably the last fat woman on earth would go to the trouble."

Three of us hurried off into the kitchen to get the fat woman her foodstuffs, to get it quick. When we came back in again she was again talking about that elephant. Indian elephants, African elephants, white elephants, she said, they are not the same thing. They are about a zillion miles different one from the other, as different as your personal skills are from each other's, and then another zillion different from the elephant you might see in the zoo. "You want to hear about how to manage your interpersonal skills, I know you do, but I've gone flat in the face from talking about it. So listen close. I'm not going to repeat myself. You take a man from New York or one from Cleveland or the West Coast and they roll over on you, *you* tell me the difference. You tell me. It's all *their* business they are interested in, and you tell me it isn't so. You do, you tell me they aren't, and I'm heading right back up the turnpike.

"You, young man," she said, pointing to Roger. "You go out into the kitchen and do something about those shoes."

She was leaning practically out of the chair. The chair legs were about six inches into the carpet. She was a very big woman.

"Get out," she said to him. "God, you ought to be ashamed of yourself.

"Come to think of it, you probably are. Probably you all are and that's why I'm here, but what I want to say is that you are all ashamed for the wrong reasons. And you want to know what else I think? I think you're proud of what shames you. I think you're ferocious in the protecting of it. I think you'd be lost without it. I think you'd maim neighbor and friend just to keep it intact. I think you know that if you somehow got rid of your shame there wouldn't be a damn thing left. You'd be a sizzling pile on the floor.

"Somebody make that asshole move," she said. "Make him go and clean those shoes."

But no one did, and Roger was squirming. You could see him working himself up to a level of defiance. It was her job, I guess, to get him to that point. Maybe to get us all there.

I was yawning. My legs had gone to sleep. My arms, too. I couldn't stop yawning, and now she saw it, and I thought she smiled at me.

I felt like the teacher's pet, and liked the feeling, though I kept on yawning. I wasn't even trying to disguise the yawns now.

Roger stood up, shoving his chair back. "I'm not going anywhere," he said. "Whatever is on my shoes is on my shoes because somebody put it there. No fat slob like you is going to boss me around."

"Nobody put it there," the fat woman said. "Maybe they left it somewhere but you were the one walked in it and I'd say you better clean that muck off. You better clean it off right now."

So we sat about ten minutes watching her eat her ice cream. She didn't say another word. The others started glaring at Roger and telling him not to start spoiling everything. "Just once," they said. "Consider the group's interest."

"Screw the group," Roger said.

"It's just getting interesting," they said. "No one will hold it against you or think less of you if you get the hell out of here so the rest of us can start learning something."

"Screw you," Roger said.

"Take Kathleen with you," they said. "Kathleen can keep you company in the kitchen while we go on with our assertiveness training. You know Kathleen's good company. Go on out there with him, Kathleen."

I didn't say anything. I just yawned in their faces. They all should have known I wouldn't throw water on Roger's burning house. I wouldn't raise the alarm even to save his children. They could all dry up and be blown to hell before I'd go out into the kitchen with Roger. I patted my feet against the carpet and yawned and felt nothing.

The fat woman ate her ice cream. She looked at us like we were elephants sitting on her.

She was a black woman. I'd hardly been aware of it until that minute. Whenever she moved the chair moved, she was that much stuffed into it.

We all listened to the clock. She was getting paid about five dollars the minute and she was supposed to be good. It was said of her that she could get any house in order.

"Roger?" someone said.

You know how the community works its will on you. A minute later I was out in the kitchen with Roger and Roger was looking at his shoes.

"There's nothing on my shoes," he said. "Who does that fat bitch think she is telling me to clean my shoes?"

I yawned. I could barely lift my arm. I could feel the barest trickle inside. "Here's a knife," I said. "Scrape off the muck. Unless you think it's all inside, then scrape it off and shut up."

"If it's inside somebody else put it there," he said. "I didn't have a hand in it."

"You've got hands in it up to your elbows," I said. "You're stirring it about and ladling it up into everyone's soup bowls every chance you get."

Roger didn't balk. He stepped up and pressed me against the counter and ran his hand up under my blouse and ran his hands up and down my back and kept pressing against me.

"Don't do that, Roger," I said, but he went on doing just that. I didn't like his hands on my skin but what I liked less was the cold air on my backside and that numbness in my legs. If he backed up I thought I'd wilt right down to the floor. "Cut it out, Roger," I said.

"Screw you," he said. He had his face rolling about at my throat and my blouse all the way up to my neck. I was draped up against him and if he let go I knew I would fall, though I felt some tingle in my toes and I was able now to clench my hands.

"I'm mortally wounded," he said. "She got me square between the eyes."

I yawned, and looked over at the ice cream in the carton melting by the sink. I looked at the wine bottles arrayed on the counter, open and not open, and a cork down on the floor. I'd had one glass earlier and it made me sick.

"No more of this Mr. Nice Guy," Roger said. "From here on, I'm taking charge."

I yawned about a dozen times, leaning back against the sink, not even bothering to cover my mouth. I wanted to sit down, or lie down, just crumple up with a pillow over my head. I was still feeling sick. I'd been feeling sick for about six months now, which was why I'd enrolled at the Institute in the first place.

"I'm going to be your mission control center," Roger said. "I'm going to be everybody's mission control." He had such a nasty expression on his face it made me sick to look at him. He reminded me of every man I'd ever had in my life, and I had the sudden, weary feeling that something terrible was about to happen.

"I hate you," Roger said. "I fucking hate all you women."

He backed up and I felt myself starting to slide, to crumple to the floor, but he stuck both hands into my waist and yanked and lifted me and my jean-front burst open.

"Jesus Christ!" I said. And I just rolled my eyes. I rolled them and rolled them and it was like Jupiter among the rainclouds. He'd snatched my zipper into two halves.

"Jesus Christ!" I said. I reached over and grabbed a wine bottle by the neck and I tapped it lightly against the top of Roger's head. But I was in control. I wasn't worried. I wasn't numb in my limbs anymore.

"Here's a warning, Roger," I said. "Here's the only warning you will get." And I clenched my hand and put my fist up under his nose and I pushed hard.

He scooted back, holding his nose.

I watched blood seep between his fingers and trickle down his wrist.

Then he spun about and darted away into the mop closet off the kitchen and hid.

I walked out into the yard and all the trees were strung with popcorn ropes and lit up like Christmas, about a million of these trees, and behind them the Institute's big red neon saying Development Institute, and behind that a crimson wipe over the city like it had burned last night and was still smoldering and would go on smoldering for a billion years because all the firemen and all the citizens were out on strike.

There was someone sitting in the boughs of one of the trees, coughing to get my attention, and when I got nearer I saw it was my mother, Geraldine.

"I'm not really here, Kate," she said. "You're hallucinating."

"I know it," I said. "I'm not that far gone."

She had on a white nightgown, a scarf of some transparency covering her hair, and she was sipping a McDonald's milkshake through a straw.

"Why don't you come home?" she said.

"I never hurt you," she said.

"We were all young in those days," she said.

"If I made mistakes they were mostly little ones and done in innocence," she said.

"If you're sick," she said, "come home. Come back to where people love you. Get on the turnpike tonight."

She slurped at her milkshake, staring at me over the brim. Through the trees I could see the crimson wipe over the city and her red face and the striations of red in her garment.

"You're not sick anyway," she said. "What you're suffering is no more than a long depression. What you need is a mission in your life."

"Be quiet, Mom," I said.

She plucked something from the chest of her gown and threw it down at me.

"Fix yourself up, honey," she said. "You look a disgrace."

I picked up from the dirt the safety pin she'd thrown.

"I was never thin," she said, "like you or like that woman in there.

"I wouldn't know an elephant from Adam," she said, "not even if it sat on me. The only man I ever let get on top of me was your father and the truth is I was mostly on top of him. I was underneath or on top, I tell you, for nearly the whole of our years, and you can like it or lump it.

"Your pants are a mess," she said. "You are going to have to throw those out, since you can't sew.

"But I never could either," she said.

I said, "Mom, go home," and she did, or went some place, and the next instant it was my father sitting in the very boughs she'd sat in, smoking his pipe, or lighting it and puffing, and lighting it again and puffing, just the way he'd always done. He had on his blue pajamas with all the burnt holes.

"Kathleen, Kathleen," he said. "Kathleen Geraldine?" And I waited for him to say more, though he didn't. He kept relighting his pipe, and smoking, and fumbling in his pockets for more matches.

I had never been able to talk to him in the flesh, and the hallucination was no easier.

Funny thing, that. You'd think I'd be willing to say whatever I wanted to people so silly they'd sit in trees.

"What is this place?" he said. "Some kind of hospital?"

I said yes, and he nodded, and disappeared.

I barged back into the house and there was Roger still huddled up in the mop closet with his bleeding nose. I went on through the assembly room into the bathroom, without looking at the fat woman or anyone else, but the one stool was occupied so I squatted down beside the person seated there and peed on the tiles.

"I know you," she said. "You're the God-almighty's daughter."

I said, "Which one?"

She reeled off the names of a half-dozen God-almighties, and I kept on peeing. The urine rode up past my shoes and kept going. Finally I was done and the woman rolled off tissue and passed it down to me.

"You're cute," she said, "but still there will be retribution."

When she was gone I bolted the door and those milling outside in the wait of their turn wailed and struck their fists against the door.

I took off my Levi's and held the crotch up to the mirror. The zipper was all bent and wrecked. He'd ripped my white panties too and the cloth just sagged over my stomach.

"I'll buy a new zipper," I said, "and sew the son of a bitch on."

There was pandemonium outside, three or four people rattling the door.

I threw the panties in the rubbish and put back on my jeans and used Mom's pin to hold the waist.

I washed my face and examined it in the mirror and gave cursory look for another exit. But there wasn't one, nothing I could squeeze through, so I opened the door and plowed hurriedly through the throng. "Watch where you walk," I said to them. "Some helpless creature has wet the floor."

I looked in on Roger who was still huddled in the mop closet, shivering and crying, and I passed a wad of tissue down to him.

"Stop it," I said. "Pick up your bones and go outside, there are fathers and mothers and all kinds of people up in the trees."

The fat woman was talking about the days when she was thin and the gang was gathered on the floor around her chair, saying, yeah, yeah, yeah, and mentioning their various adversities and afflictions, and though I liked the fat woman well enough I felt like shunning the lot of them.

Through the window I saw Roger out in the neon-lit yard talking to the people in the trees.

"You," the fat woman said. "You at the window. Go out to the kitchen and get me a pan of hot sudsy water, a dry towel, and a dish cloth. Bring the pan to me and put it in my lap."

"Why?" I asked.

She smiled at me and at everybody else in the room.

"'Why' is a good question," she said. "Under the circumstances, it's the best question she could have asked." She stopped smiling. "Just do it," she said.

I did it. I ran the water and got it nice, hot and sudsy, and I put it in her lap.

"And you tell me she's sick," the woman said to the group. "Yet you'll note she knew when to stop asking why and when she did it she did it with zest. Now," she said to me. "Kneel down here between my legs."

I did so.

"Which do you want?" she said. "Wash or wipe?"

"Wash," I said.

She nodded. "Good. I like washing best too. Wiping, you're so much at the mercy of that other's pace, which is a position to avoid unless you've got full trust in your partner or don't mind standing by twiddling your thumbs.

"You've all been thumb-twiddlers, I can see that."

I washed her ice-cream dish and her spoon and Coke glass, while she dried them squeaky clean.

"That's good," she said. "Now somebody go and empty this mess. This here woman and me, we're not stooping to such menial tasks."

They did so.

"The thing about your assertiveness training," the fat woman said, "is first you've got to figure out what you've got worth asserting. If you've got nothing then you go away and commune with yourself and figure out how you've come up so empty and what you can devise of value to put in its place. Until you can do that, then be content to stay a stick-in-the-mud.

"Get up now," she told me. "You know I'm done with you."

I got up.

"Mind you don't pop that pin," she said. "And me, I always carry an extra set of drawers in my purse.

"Somebody ask me some time when I'm in the right mood, and I'll tell you what else I carry.

"Somebody bring me a new pan of that warm water," the fat woman said. "I want to bathe my feet in it a while."

I looked through the window and saw Roger out in the yard still conversing with his tree people. He'd pulled a chair up. He was showing them his shoes.

Someone brought the pan of water and placed it on the

33

floor in front of the fat woman and she took off her shoes and sloshed both feet into the pan.

"Which one of you wants to sit in my lap," I heard the fat woman say, and I glanced her way and saw she was smiling at everyone in the room.

"The severe cases first," she said.

"Come on," she said. "You can each have your turn."

And the first one climbed into her lap and made as though to suckle there.

I went out into the yard and I said to Roger, "Roger, I'm taking your car."

He threw me the keys.

I got into Roger's car and got the engine going and my feet on the pedals and I got the car moving, thinking that once I hit a solid speed I would find the turnpike and once on the turnpike it would come to me where I was going and why.

"It's about a three-day drive," I heard someone say, and I looked in the rear-view mirror and there intertwined on the back seat were my mother and father smiling at me. "Three days," my father said. "So we'd best make ourselves comfortable."

"How's the gas?" he asked.

"A full tank," I said.

They curled up together, their eyes closed, and I motored on. The streets were tinged with red but overhead was a clabbered, lifting sky.

If those two are here with me, I thought, why am I bothering to go home?

"For the change of environment," I said. "There comes a time in a girl's life when her whole history advances the notion that only a change of environment will save her life. Is that where I am now?"

But they didn't hear me. They were cuddled up with each other, and snoozing, all settled in for the long miles.

Sweethearts

Hey, Sweetheart, come on over. She calls me on the phone, that's what she says. Hey, Sweetheart, come on over. I say, It's late, baby, you come over here. So we argue about it. She says, But I was over there last week. I was over there last night. Wasn't I over there last night? We argue about that. I say, Was it last night? Are you sure it was last night? She says, Wait now, I could be wrong. I could be. What's your name anyhow? That's what she says: What's your name anyhow? And we argue about my name. We argue about her name. We argue about everything under the sun. She says, If you are going to argue I don't want to talk to you. I say, Talk to me. I've got to talk to someone. She says, Sweetheart, now you're talking. I'll be right over. I'll hop into a cab. Okay, I think, that settles it. She's coming. Don't get in a sweat. She'll be here pronto. Then I say, Will you spend all night? Will you? Can I count on that? And she says, Are you kidding? All night? Have you lost your senses? What about my kids? What about my toothbrush? What about all the nights I did spend all night and nothing ever happened? What about that? I say, Hold on. Hold on, I say, I think you've got the wrong party. Let's check that number again. Do we know each other? She says, If that's how you feel I'm not coming. She says, If that's how you feel you can call somebody else. I say, what I say is, Who called who? What I say is, I don't recall ringing your number. What I say is, Sweetheart, this isn't working out. She says, Whose fault is that, if I may ask you? Who started this? You always want to argue. Why do you always want to argue? You'd better get straight with yourself before you want to start making time with a woman like me. Am I making time? I say, Is that what I'm doing? I say, How much time am I making if you come over and nothing happens? She says, Did I say that? Did I? So we argue about what happens and what does not happen. We argue at considerable length about that. We are shouting into the phone and she says, Why are you shouting? Stop shouting, get a grip on yourself. But things have gone too far, I can't get a grip on myself. I can't get straight with myself. She says, I know. I know, that has always been your trouble. I say, What trouble? I wasn't in any trouble until I met you. She says, You're right. I don't doubt that for a minute. She says, I'm always trouble, I've been trouble for every man I've ever known. What I say is, No, you haven't. I say, You're a life saver, that's what you are. Thank you, she says. Thank you. It is very nice of you to say that. Even if you don't mean it, it is nice of you to say so. I mean it, I say. You've saved my life a thousand times. She says, If only I could believe that. If only we could start over. I say, Every time I see you is a new start, every time, even if nothing happens. She says, Oh God, what can I do? What can I say? When I say nothing happens I don't mean it the way you think I mean it. My head's in a whirl, that's what she says. I say, Tell me about it. She says, I can't talk now. She says, I've got to see you, what I want to say can't be said on the phone. We're in deep water, she says. How did we get in such deep water? I say, Let's talk about it. Okay, she says, okay. I'll be right over and we can talk about it, although that's all we do, is talk about it. Do you really think we should? What I say is, Yes, yes, we owe it to each other. Fine, she says, I'm on my way. Shall I pack my toothbrush? Shall I stay the night? Can we have a nice friendly dinner somewhere? The truth is I haven't eaten, I haven't eaten in days and days. I say, Same here. I say, God, I'm starving, let's do that, let's eat somewhere. She says, Good, good, I can't wait to see you. I think to myself, God, what a shot, what a woman! I can't wait to see her, that's what I think. Wear a jacket, she says, it's cold, it's very cold out there. You too, I say. Dress warmly, don't let the cold get next to your bones. She says, You know what I want next to my bones, don't you, don't you, you've always known. I say, Hurry, let's not waste any time, why have we been wasting all this time? I'm on my way, she says, I'm flying out of the door. Me, too, I say, goodbye for now. Goodbye, she says, kiss-kiss, she says, into the phone. What a woman, I think, why are you always fighting with her? No fighting, I say, anymore. Get straight with yourself, Jack, go to a nice restaurant, hold her hands, look into her eyes, get lost inside her eyes. Get inside her coat with her, run your hands over her body, warm each other, let the flesh commingle, be bone against bone, the bones in harvest, go at it breath to breath, breath with breath, forget this ashes to ashes business, just forget it. Hold her, lock eyes, get inside that coat with her. And don't stop there. Why stop there? Call the children in. Say, Children, do we have news for you! Say, Children, gather around, assemble your bedrolls, for we have important announcements to make. The world does not belong to those whom you thought it belonged to. No, it doesn't. You see this coat? Come, get inside this coat with us, let's hug each other, warm each other. Look into our eyes. Did we say "lost"? We don't mean "lost," we mean "found," as in "Eureka!" as in "Boy oh boy!" as in "new continents," "larger horizons," "greater expectations," "warmer seasons," "fabled heights," etc., you get the idea. The world doesn't belong to those you thought it belonged to, and never did. Say that, I tell myself. Tell them that. Get your act in gear. So I go down and I wait for her cab, I wait for it. She's my sweetheart, I am hers. We are sweethearts to each other, we are lovers through thick and thin. She'll be here soon, any minute now, any second now. You believe me, don't you? Accept it, every word is true. There's her cab now, turning the corner, a nice yellow one. I can see the driver, I can see her in the back seat, black coat up around her ears. Come on now, hurry, hurry it up. I want to get inside that coat with you, I want to look into your eyes, to lock hearts, to say, Cabbie, turn this cab around. Cabbie, haven't you heard the news? We've got everything, we've got all we need. What you have here, in this neighborhood, on this freezing night, are two people, two sweethearts, who utterly desire, comprehend, and complete each other. Snow? You call this snow? This isn't snow, this isn't a freeze. We're trim and fit and ready for anything.

Art

I told the woman I wanted that bunch down near the pine grove by the rippling stream.

Where the cow is? she asked.

I told her yep, that was the spot.

She said I'd have to wait until the milking was done.

The cow mooed a time or two as we waited. It was all very peaceful.

How much if you throw in the maiden? I asked.

Without the cow? she asked, or *with*?

Both would be nice, I said.

But it turned out a Not For Sale sign had already gone up on the girl. Too bad. it was sweet enough with her out of the picture, but not quite the same.

I took my cut bunch of flowers and plodded on behind the cow over to the next field. I wanted a horse too, if I could get one cheap.

Any horses? I asked.

Not today, they said.

Strawberries?

Not the season, I was told.

At home, I threw out the old bunch and put the new crop in a vase by the picture window so the wife might marvel at them when she came in from her hard day's grind.

I staked the cow out front where the grass was still doing pretty well.

It was touch-and-go, whether we'd be able to do the milking ourselves. It would be rough without a shed or stall.

Oh, hand-painted! the wife said when she came in.

I propped her up in the easy chair and put up her feet. She looked a trifle wind-blown.

Hard day? I asked.

So-so, she said.

I mixed up a gin and tonic, nice as I knew how, and lugged that in.

A touch flat, she said, but the lemon wedge has a nice effect.

I pointed out the cow, which was tranquilly grazing.

Sweet, she said. Very sweet. What a lovely idea.

I put on the stereo for her.

That needle needs re-doing, she observed. The tip needs retouching, I mean.

It will have to wait until tomorrow, I told her.

She gave me a sorrowful look, though one without any dire reproach in it. She pecked me a benign one on the cheek. A little wet. I wiped it off before it could do any damage.

The flowers were a good thought, she said. I appreciate the flowers.

Well, you know how it is, I said. What I meant was that one did the best one could – though I didn't really have to tell her that. It was what she was always telling me.

She was snoozing away in the chair as I tiptoed off to bed.

I was beginning to flake a little myself. Needed a good touch-up job from an expert.

We all do, I guess. The dampness, the mildew, the rot – it gets into the system somehow.

Not much to be done about it, however.

I thought about the cow. Wondered if I hadn't made a mistake on that. Without the maiden to milk her, there didn't seem to be much *point* in having a cow. Go back tomorrow, I thought. Offer a good price for the maiden, the stream, and the whole damned field.

Of course, I could go the other way: find a nice seascape somewhere. Hang that up.

Well, sleep on it, I thought.

The wife slipped into bed about two in the morning. That's approximate. The paint job on the hour hand wasn't holding up very well. The undercoating was beginning to show through on the entire clock face, and a big crack was developing down in the six o'clock area.

Shoddy goods, I thought. Shoddy artisanship.

Still, we'd been around a bit. Undated, unsigned, but somewhere in the nineteenth century was my guess. It was hard to remember. I just wished the painter had been more careful. I wished he'd given me more chest, and made the bed less rumpled.

Sorry, baby, she said. Sorry I waked you.

She whispered something else, which I couldn't hear, and settled down far away on her side of the bed. I waited for her to roll into me and embrace me. I waited for her warmth, but she remained where she was and I thought all this very strange.

What's wrong? I said.

She stayed very quiet and did not move. I could feel her

holding herself in place, could hear her shallow, irregular breathing, and I caught the sweep of one arm as she brought it up to cover her face. She started shivering.

I am so sorry, she said. I am so sorry. She said that over and over.

Tell me what's wrong, I said.

No, she said, please don't touch me, please don't, please don't even think about touching me. She went on like this for some seconds, her voice rising, growing in alarm, and I thought to myself: Well, I have done something to upset her, I must have said or done something unforgivable, and I lay there with my eyes open wide, trying to think what it might be.

I am so sorry, she said. So very very sorry.

I reached for her hand, out of that hurting need we have for warmth and reassurance, and it was then that I found her hand had gone all wet and muddy and smeary.

Don't! she said, oh please don't, I don't want you to hurt yourself!

Her voice was wan and low and she had a catch in her voice and a note of forlorn panic. I lifted my hand away quickly from her wetness, though not quickly enough for I knew the damage already had been done. The tips of my fingers were moist and cold, and the pain, bad enough but not yet severe, was slowly seeping up my arm.

My drink spilled, she said. She snapped that out so I would know.

Christ, I thought. Oh Jesus Christ. God help us.

I shifted quickly away to the far side of the bed, my side, away from her, far as I could get, for I was frightened now and all I could think was that I must get away from her, I must not let her wetness touch me any more than it had.

Yes, she said shivering, do that, stay there, you must try and save yourself, oh darling I am so sorry.

We lay in the darkness, on our backs, separated by all that distance, yet I could still feel her warmth and her tremors and I knew there was nothing I could do to save her.

Her wonderful scent was already going and her weight on the bed was already decreasing.

I slithered up high on the sheets, keeping my body away from her, and ran my good hand through her hair and down around her warm neck and brought my face up against hers.

I know it hurts, I said. You're being so brave.

Do you hurt much? she said. I am so terribly, terribly sorry. I was dozing in the chair and opened my eyes and saw the dark shape of the cow out on the lawn and for an instant I didn't know what it was and it scared me. I hope I haven't hurt you. I've always loved you and the life we had in here. My own wounds aren't so bad now. I don't feel much of anything anymore. I know the water has gone all through me and how frightful I must look to you. Oh please forgive me, it hurts and I'm afraid I can't think straight.

I couldn't look at her. I looked down at my own hand and saw that the stain had spread. It had spread up to my elbow and in a small puddle where my arm lay, but it seemed to have stopped there. I couldn't look at her. I knew her agony must be very great and I marveled a little that she was being so brave for I knew that in such circumstances I would be weak and angry and able to think only of myself.

Water damage, I thought, that's the hardest part to come to terms with. The fear that's over you like a curse. Every day you think you've reconciled yourself to it and come to terms with how susceptible you are, and unprotected you are, and then something else happens. But you never think you will do it to yourself.

Oil stands up best, I thought. Oh holy Christ why couldn't we have been done in oil.

You get confident, you get to thinking what a good life you have, so you go out and buy yourself flowers and a goddamn cow.

I wish I could kiss you, she moaned. I wish I could.

My good hand was already behind her neck and I wanted to bring my head down on her breasts and put my hand there too. I wanted to close my eyes and stroke her all over and lose myself in the last sweetness I'd ever know.

I will too, I thought. I'll do it.

Although I tried, I couldn't, not all over, so I stroked my hand through her hair and rolled my head over till my lips gently touched hers.

She sobbed and broke away.

It's too much, she said. I'm going to cry. I am, I know I am.

Don't, I said. Don't. If you do that will be the end of you.

The tears burst and I spun above her, wrenching inside, gripping the sheet and wiping it furiously about her eyes.

I can't stop it! she said. It's no use. It burns so much but I can't stop it, it's so sad but I've got to cry!

She kept on crying.

Soon there was just a smear of muddled color on the pillow where her face had been, and then the pillow was washing away.

The moisture spread, reaching out and touching me, filling the bed until at last it and I collapsed on the floor.

Yet the stain continued widening.

I had the curious feeling that people were already coming in, that someone already was disassembling our frame, pressing us flat, saying, Well here's one we can throw out. You can see how the house, the cow, etc., have all bled together. You can't recognize the woman anymore, or see that this once was a bed and . . . well it's all a big puddle except those flowers. Flowers are a dime a dozen but these are pretty good, we could snip out the flowers, I guess, give them their own small frame. Might fetch a dollar or two, what do you say?

Regeneration

You think I'm talking about loneliness, isolation, loss of hope, about incongruity, split seams, the disrepair of relationships, or perhaps about no more than the simple passage of time, innocence gone, possibilities deferred, about a gate that opened and never closed, but there is more to talk about than that. Agnes came in, she was downcast, her hair wet, her knees limp, she said, "I don't know what happened. I had my shoes on, then they were lost, they slipped off my feet at some point and afterwards I could not find them anywhere."

"Here your shoes are," I said, and of course I had to explain. You find shoes, you know to whom they belong, you bring them home, you put them up on the radiator to dry, you say, "Here they are."

"Well, how did they get there?" she says, and you explain exactly where it was on the street that you found them, and she says, "How absurd, I was never in such a place, no never, how strange!"

And for my money you leave it there. You go to bed, sleep, rise early, have breakfast, and do not speak of the matter for weeks and weeks, for years and years. It is all forgotten, suddenly both of you are very old, and one day she says out of the blue, "I wonder whatever happened to those grand old shoes I used to have, I haven't seen them in years," and you think, "Ah, lost a second time," and it starts all over again.

Now that's how it is with shoes. Let's this time consider hats. She had this most wonderful hat, most elegant, a most splendid fur, lost I think it was on a train in London, England, midnight ride on the Tube, and someone called up one day, said, "Is your name by any chance Agnes ———, and are you by chance missing a hat?"

Oh yes! you say.

And they bring it around, you have a drink together, offer rewards which are refused, and you compliment each other. You say, "Yes, that's the hat all right, how wonderful, we'd given up on that rascal forever."

So that's hats.

But what of neckties, handkerchiefs, scarves, salt and pepper shakers, pots and pans – entire households, total personalities! – what of them?

"Excuse me, sir, haven't I met you somewhere before?"

"Oh now wait a minute, aren't you a friend of so and so's, didn't I meet you in such and such a place five years ago?"

"Do you have a cousin named Prince, by any chance?"

"Ever been in Flanders?"

"Wasn't Nero a pip?"

What is your answer to this? Do you simply carry on, content to let such mysteries spin and spin? Offer an exchange of handshakes, smile merrily or dourly, and go on with your life?

"What? Yes? You've located a hidden race, you say? Hitherto unknown? Why, my dear fellow, I'm not at all surprised! No, by all means, bring them around. I'll have my footman meet you at the gate."

But of course you do not send your footman since this person does not exist, and instead you go yourself. You are there by the open gate waiting, wondering who will show, what noble or ignoble creatures this stranger will bring, and if no one comes, if you are still waiting long after midnight, walking the stones after all such traffic has long ceased, then what's the loss?

Oh the question's easy; it's only that you know, and for-ever will know, that something is to come, and so you wait on, studying the empty street, made moody by the dancing shade, wishing to hell Agnes had never lost her shoes, but kind of grateful, you know, that this and that contact paid off.

The Willies

The boy's name was Willie; his parents she called Willie too, Mizz Willie, Mr. Willie, the Willies. "Mizz Willie, can Willie play with me?" Willie could or couldn't; most days he didn't want to. He was awfully hard to love, Willie was, but she did. Drab days, those No-Willie Days, those Willie-won't-play-with-me days. Oh, like a big toothache, those days. But Willie was all she had. No other children lived on her street, younger or older. Willie was the whole show and days without Willie, well, you could try sitting in the kitty-litter box. A cat, yes, but the cat was old. The cat had retired from life. It had blind eyes and wouldn't scratch or roll over or run. It wasn't Willie, that cat.

Willie lived by the telephone, eternally awaiting calls. Calls from the dead, he said, it was how the dead communed with people. Though, sitting at his feet, she never heard the phone ring. "The cord," Willie said, making her move, "the cord has to be straight." He would make her move, and move again, and wait for the phone to ring. "Don't you sweat it," he said. "They'll call. They said they would." The dead were up to no good, she thought. They were off places having fun.

Willie's face was brutal. He would make nasty, brutal

faces, and twist her foot. "This leg," he'd say, "I could snap it, one two three. I'm strong. I'm big. I could sit on you and all the air would squeeze out of you. It would go up, up in this room, and lift the ceiling. That's what I could do with you, lift the ceiling. You want me to try?" She would whimper when Willie sat on her, and whimper when he twisted her leg. "You better be quiet," Willie would say. "You try yelling and you'll get thrown out of here. We don't allow yelling in this house." She would go blue in the face, blue with the hurt, but he would go on sitting on her. The ceiling wouldn't lift. You would see it wrinkle a bit, wrinkle and roll, but it wouldn't lift. "I could blow out that window," Willie said. "I could huff and puff and blow that window out. I could. That's what causes hurricanes, all that huffing and puffing, a million people, but none can do it how I can."

Willie was rough. He was very rough, and even his faces could make her cry. He was heavy and could flatten her. "Flatten you and roll you up," he said, "the way you would a carpet. I could if I wanted to." "Can't," she'd say. "Can't." That was always her mistake, saying "Can't. Can not." Because what else could she say? And of course Willie would try. There was nothing Willie wouldn't try. Willie had the run of the house and could do whatever he wanted to. Though he never would come outside. "Nah," he'd say. "I don't want to go out there. Everything I want is right in here. You'd be crazy to want to play out there." But children did. She knew they did. She would tell Willie of children she had seen playing in the streets, up on swings in parks, in playgrounds – things she'd seen herself while going about town in her mother's car – but Willie would say, "Nah." "Nah, that's a lie. You made that up. You're not fooling me." "Just for that," he'd say, "I'm going to twist your leg." Willie was stronger than she. He knew just how to twist it, and twist it harder, if you screamed. "That'll show you," he'd say. "Nobody messes with me."

Willie was all she had. It was Willie or nothing, or sometimes driving with her mother in the car. Often, for no reason, Willie would suddenly reach out and pull her hair. A big yank. The first few times she screamed and Mizz Willie came running and the next minute she was standing outside the Willie door blinking at sunlight so sharp it stabbed the eyes. "Go home," Mizz Willie said. "Go home now. If you can't play peacefully together, in peace and tranquility, then you can march straight home, young woman." Mizz Willie called her "young woman" and "Missycat" and "poor thing," and other names such as "Little Yew." Mizz Willie said she ought to have more skin on her bones and stand straighter and do something about her stringy hair. Mizz Willie also said she had "the funniest knees." But Mizz Willie often said little to her except when she came running or when she pushed her out of the door.

Mr. Willie "had a condition" and was rarely to be seen. "You can say that to me, in your condition?" Mizz Willie would say to him. Or: "If I were in your condition . . ." Or: "The condition you're in, I'm not surprised." Though to "Little Yew's" mind, Mr. Willie looked ordinary enough. He was tall, and stooped a lot, and usually had a glass of something in his hand. The way he stooped, it was like some giant bird had him by the claws, transporting him to some high abode. He had the same ketchupy face as Willie did when he was twisting her foot. He wore a green bathrobe, and mostly what you noticed about him was his white wrinkled feet with the toes that swam up over each other. Mr. Willie called her "Tiger" and "Cutup" and "Mustard," she didn't know why. The one time Mr. Willie had ever tried really to talk to her he had said, "When was it your father died? Was it a long time ago?" But that too was a long time ago.

She liked riding with her mother. Those were good, very good, days. Such very good, wondrous, days. Not long ago they'd gone on a picnic, little wicker basket on a white sheet by a tree in the park, and her mother had said, "Such a shame your friend Willie couldn't come. Tell me about Willie. Is he awfully nice?"

That day she'd asked her mother the same question Mr. Willie had asked her: When did my father die? Her mother had looked so amazed. "Oh, he isn't dead," she said. "He just went away. But that was a long time ago. He could be dead, of course. He *could* be. He was so mean, and such a pushy fellow, and always getting himself into such hot water, that someone very well might have killed him by now.

"Yes, they very well might have. I always told him some day they would."

Mizz Willie said, "Don't you have a home?" She said, "Where do you live, poor thing?" She said, "I bet your mother, if you have one, isn't as good-looking as I am. I bet she's never been swept off her feet the way I have." Mizz Willie didn't like to hear others speak. She'd interrupt at the first word and say whatever was on her mind to continue saying. She'd say to Willie, "Are you talking to the dead again? Well, that's all right. No harm in that. Are you waiting for the phone to ring? Well, I won't answer it. They have nothing to say to me. Just tell them I inquired. Tell them I wish them their honest best." Sometimes Mr. Willie or Mizz Willie would walk through the room when Willie was squeezing her, or twisting her leg, and they would not even look down. They would step over Willie, or over her, and float on to whatever business was engaging them.

One day the phone did ring, as Willie's arm was around

her neck, choking her. Willie's arm went slack. He was shocked, and let it ring and ring. Then he choked her harder, so much harder, and to "Little Yew's" way of thinking, that day, well, that day, the ceiling really was lifting. She clawed at his arm, she squirmed, she kicked; Willie's grunts, his breath, were in her ear. "It's them," he said. "I told you." She couldn't speak. One arm was choking her, the other twisting her head.

"Get the phone, Willie," Mizz Willie called. But Willie let it go on ringing. He crawled off her and wriggled up next to the sofa as though he would crawl under it if he could. His mouth was open and his eyes so big. He was shaking. His face was white at that moment, not scarlet anymore. That was her biggest surprise: that Willie was such a scaredy-cat.

You could see the little table jitter every time the phone rang. "Get the phone, Willie," Mizz Willie called. Willie struck out and knocked the phone to the floor. You could hear someone talking over it, low, and as though from a great many rumbly miles. The voice was raspy, and rather hollowed out. Willie snatched up the receiver and held it briefly at his ear. Willie's eyes went so large. His breathing seemed to stop. He didn't want to talk to the dead, that much was clear. But he wanted her to. He scooted over and pressed the phone against her ear, pressed hard, so that her ear flattened. It hurt. "Little Yew" was trying to get her breath back. She was rubbing her throat and neck and trying not to cry too loud. But she listened. She listened, and then she slapped Willie's hand away and held the phone herself. She nodded a few times. She got herself comfortable. Then she too began to speak. "Yes," she said, "that's very interesting. Willie was just doing that to me." And she waited until the voice had said again whatever it was it had to say. "I know," she said. "I feel that way too, sometimes. Does it ever end? Is it always so horrible?" The voice went on, and she went on listening to it. She listened for a long time. "Where ARE you?" she asked. And she listened to the answer to that. "Wow, I'll bet!" she said. "I'll bet you're sorry now." Willie, watching her, clearly wanted the phone himself now. He was so eager, reaching for the phone. But she kept darting away. She said to Willie at one point, "Don't step on the cord! You've got to keep it straight!"

Mr. and Mizz Willie came into the room after a while, and they too watched her talking to the dead. "Do you know my father?" she asked. "Is he missing me?" "Wait," she said at last, "I'll give you MY number. You can call me there." She gave it, in just the order in which her mother had taught it to her, and hung up.

And after that, she said goodbye to the Willies, the last time she ever would. She went home and never saw the Willies ever again, in her life or theirs.

Red Meat

When Mary Lamb was a young child she had a friend for a time, named Sookie, who lived far across town, although the two went to the same school. Sookie came and went as she liked, traveling by bicycle, or by bus or trolley when she had the money, and Mary Lamb never knew when Sookie might appear at her door.

One evening in winter Sookie showed up as the Lambs were eating dinner, and though she sat at the table with them she did not eat anything. Mary Lamb would remember this, because of the intense, all but confrontational way Sookie stared at her father, and because her father, often a difficult man, kept insisting that Sookie should eat something. "Get rid of that starved look," he told Sookie. "Put some of this red meat in your mouth."

Mary Lamb could not recall now what plates had been on the table, but she saw that Sookie studied the dishes with an emotion close to venom, when she was not scowling at her father.

After dinner Sookie asked Mary Lamb if she wanted to go for a walk, which her parents thought curious, since it was so cold. But in the end they saw nothing wayward or remiss in the notion, so long as the two children bundled up warmly.

"You do have a good coat, don't you?" Mary Lamb's father said to Sookie. "Why did you come out in this weather without a good muffler? Where are your boots?"

Mary Lamb could not now remember what coats they had worn that evening, or where exactly they had walked, though she did not think it far. Nor did she recall many of the things they must have talked about, since Sookie was ever running on about something.

She does know that at one point Sookie clutched her arm and proclaimed, with a viciousness Mary Lamb found alarming, "Your *father* is in *government!*"

They came to a deserted house and Sookie suggested they go inside and explore. In Mary Lamb's mind this was possibly dangerous, and certainly against the law, as signs about the property clearly stated. "I don't want to get into trouble," she told Sookie. But her friend persisted. By then, anyway, they were already inside, and Sookie struck a match, and then lit a stub of candle, which she had been carrying all this while secreted in a pocket. Rather, Mary Lamb thought, as though this entry into the deserted house had been Sookie's intention from the beginning.

Mary Lamb followed Sookie's footsteps down rotted stairs into a cold and damp basement, and here they heard something ferociously growling. In that second Sookie blew out their candle, immersing them in total darkness. Mary Lamb froze in her tracks, too frightened either to cry out or run.

"It is a dog," Sookie said, and Mary Lamb knew that she knew that, although she did not any more know why a growling dog should be in this strange house than why she was herself.

Mary Lamb could hear splashing water and what sounded like the clink of a chain, midst the growls, and it seemed to her the dog's bite was ever closer.

When she found she could speak, she told Sookie she was frightened. She reached to touch her, but Sookie was no longer beside her. "I want to leave now," she said, all but crying.

Sookie laughed. She said, "Why? Haven't you been a good girl? Didn't you eat all the food on your plate?"

It seemed to Mary Lamb that Sookie's voice was above her, and retreating, while the dog was furiously barking.

"Didn't you make your bed this morning? Have you gone out into the cold without your good muffler? Where are your boots? Where are your boots?"

Sookie was now shouting, and the dog's wild splashing, the clinking chain, ever more menacing.

"*Weren't you nice to the dogs? Didn't you Lambs ever feed them?*"

That was all Mary Lamb heard from Sookie, except the scuff of her shoes on the stairs, and the slam of a door.

She felt the dog's breath on her legs, and then the dog's snout nudging her thighs.

She wondered how long it would be before anyone discovered the body.

On the dark street, some minutes later, shaking with chill, and ashamed of her cowardice, Mary Lamb saw two neighborhood women approaching, looking grotesquely tall in their long black coats, their feet in rubber boots that echoed as they landed.

Mary Lamb at once dived out of sight into the bushes. As the women passed, this is what she heard them say:

First woman: "Have you ever known, or lived with, a dyed-in-the-wool maniac?"

Second woman: "In Clifford, Montana."

Then the women were gone and a short while later Mary Lamb, sobbing now, crept out of her hiding place.

At home, Mary Lamb discovered her parents in the living room, listening to records on the Victrola. She snuck past their door and into her room, and for some little while lay biting her knuckles under the covers. Then she drew herself a bath and stretched out in the steaming water, atune to creaks in the floorboards and walls, the groaning messages nightly relayed in this old house some called a mansion. Her parents' long-ago songs wafted thinly up to her, her father's arrogant voice often breaking on the high notes as he sung along.

She would not have a good life, Mary Lamb thought.

She would have to exercise extreme caution.

Want to Play House?

Here. Come here. Yes. Now this is what you do. You see where I have marked with my stick that line in the dirt?

That is the back door. You come in the door and I am standing here in the kitchen. That's right, this is the kitchen, see my pots and pans? See my table?

All right, don't sulk. Look, I will draw the table in the dirt with this stick. See? That is the table. It is polished nice and clean, and it has our plates on it, and our silverware, and this nice stew I have made.

No, no, you don't sit down yet. Let me explain. You go back to the door – not yet! – and you come in with your muddy boots and you see me here at the sink where I am washing the dishes and looking out the window, and I don't see you yet. For heaven's sake? My back is turned. Do you think I have eyes in the back of my head? Use your imagination.

Very well, I will draw the sink and the windows. There. See them? Take your hands out of your pockets and pay attention.

Let me see: what am I wearing? I am wearing my dressing gown. Yes, this old quilted pattern gown like my . . . like mothers wear. It's seen better days. But I have on my stockings, and my make-up. Kind of pretty, you know. I am very pretty, and gay, but just worn out. With worry over you and the kids. I have lost my spunk. Bills, bills, bills, and I never get any help. You know, like when Grandmama died. How Grandpapa was, after that. You remember, don't you? Well, you were too young.

No, you don't whistle, you don't say anything. You have your lunch pail with you, and you just stand at the door, holding your pail in your hand, and you know I have just scrubbed the linoleum because of the sparkle. So you are there in your muddy boots, not speaking to me until I turn around and see you there. You like watching me secretly like that, because of how pretty I am and how much you love me. Why? Because I said so. That is how we play.

Now listen to me: you've got to try to look smart, and not smile, because my husband is very smart, and he almost never smiles, and his hair is combed back like this. Here, let me wet it. Yes, like that. But don't smile. Pretend you've been hard at work all day and this was just another one where you know you've not got one lick ahead, and you are in a foul mood because you know it is all my fault. I spend so much, on these pots and pans and the new linoleum – you are standing on the new linoleum, silly – and some- times you wish I was dead. Forget I said you love me, this is better.

This is much better and totally realistic. Don't you see? Because if I am dead you can start over and get yourself a new wife who will look so pretty you can't keep your hands off her. Yes, you are the Daddy. I told you, you are the Daddy. You are the Daddy and my husband. Yes, both, you can be both. Just do what I say, that's all you have to do, is what I say. Can't you see how it is done?

Okay, I will take you through it step by step, though that's precious little fun for me. I tell you, it is precious little fun for me, and I don't know why I go through it. All right, you are here at this line, which is the door, and you come in and I am sitting at the table crying my eyes out because I am full of woe.

That's right, I have changed my mind, I am not standing at the sink when you come in. Let's play this way instead. I have been full of woe all day and I have got nothing done, nothing is ever done because I am unable to rouse myself from the loathsome woe, and now I have lost all track of the time and don't know which way to turn.

Oh, which way to turn, my darling?

Forget the sink. I tell you I am at the table. Yes, weeping. I can weep really convincingly. Truly I can, so your heart would break. Now you are there, and you see me weeping. What do you do?

You don't know? Didn't I tell you? I thought you said you wanted to play. No, you can't back out now.

All right, so you hate me. That's good. You come in and what next? That's right. You put the pail on the floor, and then what?

Fine, you don't care about the polished floor. Of course you don't. I can clean it until I'm blue in the face and you never notice. Yes, do that if you want to. Sneak right up behind me and start strangling me if you want to. You won't hurt me. I'm bigger than you and I can whip your ass any day of the week. Don't think I can't. You're a worthless little limp ass and you don't scare me one little bit. Try it.

Try and hit me with that stick and you will regret it until your dying day. You are too stupid to live, do you know that? Go ahead, hit me. I dare you. I dee-double dare you. Use your rock. You think I am scared of your little rock? I'm going to whip the daylights out of you. You are being so bad I can't bear to look at you. Ugg. My skin crawls. Do it. Try that one more time and you are good as dead. You are mincemeat.

Yes. I say all that. And you are screaming, too. You are

telling me exactly what you think. It is all my fault? Understand? You would like to beat me until you can't stand up. Have you been drinking? I bet you have been drinking. I bet you have been spending all our money down at your tavern, your beer hole, and now I and the children will have to starve.

Go on, start beating. You can't hurt me. A little nothing like you couldn't hurt anyone. Such rubbish. I never saw such rubbish in my life. You are Quitsville, do you know that? You are some little rodent thing in the road I would run over. Smush you flat, you lift a hand to me. Try it. See where it gets you. You can't even earn a decent wage.

Yes.

And then I run, you see, and you chase me. You are in a rage, shouting you will kill me. Shouting how for years you have been wishing me dead.

No. No, there is no kissing. You don't have to worry one bit about kissing.

What do you mean you can't do it without real furniture?

Out here in the yard. No one can see us, you know. No one cares. No one is looking. They don't even know we are here. We can do anything we want.

Got it? Ready?

Oh, wait. I have another idea. You see here where I've drawn in the sink, the counter? And up there, the windows? Now here on the counter is this knife. Mama's butcherknife. Mine, I mean, I'm the Mama. It's under those leaves down in the dirt, where the pretend-counter is. And while you're chasing me you pick up the knife and when you catch me you stab me a thousand times. You go completely crazy and you're shouting all that stuff and stabbing me and I'm fighting back, just full of the awfullest woe, both of us, and then I will finally fall and lie still and not move a muscle because I will be dead.

Yes, pretend-dead, you'll like that part. No, in this one you are not dead, I am the dead one. Dead and gone to hell.

So you see what you have done and you roll me over in your arms and hold me. Your grief pours out. You tell me how much you love me. How sorry you are. You blubber all over the place. No, you don't have to kiss me. You rock and sob. You're sorry, so sorry you've hurt me. And you say things like this: you say how you wish we could start over. All over, fresh, and what a good time, what a wonderful life we would have. You didn't mean to hurt me. You never meant to. What went wrong? That's what you ask. You ask that a thousand times, as you rock and moan, and wish you've never been born.

Okay? That's how we do it.

Yes, let's start.

Go to the door.

You come in.

You see me weeping.

You see the knife. Already you have spotted the knife. Good. It will be so much fun.

Come on, then. Ready, set, go!

Admiral of the Fleet

When my mother saw what I was doing, with my skirt up, she said, "They are all in the films, you won't find any soldiers around here. Don't marry a soldier anyhow, unless you're in support of slaughter."

We were a thousand miles from nowhere, she said, and about the only thing one could see to marry was a useless tree stump.

We called Brad over with a Bible he'd picked up from Sunday church, and he married me to the tree stump. This was at three o'clock in the afternoon, the lemonade all gone, and a train came by and the windows looked at us. "If only we could figure a way to make that train stop here," my mother said, "we could go any place in the world we wanted to, because that's just how such journeys begin, with such small tokens of movement you hardly even know you've left your backyard."

Brad was only four years old and he went around the yard marrying everything he saw. He married the horses and the dog and cat and the cattle in the field; he married the chicken house to the chickens and the well-hole to the roped bucket and one stick to another. I walked about the yard with him, my skirt hiked so high you could see the world through it. A truck shot by on the road but it was gone before Brad could marry it to anything.

"There's sailors would marry you, they saw you like that," my mother said, though this was down at the pond on one of our walks. She said it should be an Admiral I held out for. "The Admiral of the Fleet," she said, "he would give you a good time, and maybe have some left over for me." But then we got sad and Brad wanted to go back to the house, but couldn't find his Bible. "Where *is* everybody?" Brad said, and he was looking at us while he said it, only four, but seeing we were not the same two people as those two people who had been playing marry with him. "His body is still down there," my mother said, and she began crying, because it was. "Do you know why?" she said. "Do you know why he's dead? Do you know why it happened? Do you know how? I'll tell you why and how and I don't care if I'm a crybaby or not."

Brad was crying too and I was patrolling the shore and poking at the water with a bent pole, thinking I might possibly see him down there. It hadn't been that long. It had been about three weeks, I thought, but no, my mother said, "More like four. More like four months."

And when she said that it suddenly felt to me like it could have been four years.

"You never know," my mother said. "You just never know."

"Know what?" I said, and she looked cross at me and told me to mind my own business. She said, "They are here one minute and gone the next and between those two poles is just the silliest stuff you ever heard of."

Brad wanted to go to the house but we told him to shush, and he started crying again. He'd hit us, he said, if we said anything mean like that to him again, but we didn't say it again because we were just plumb tired of talking to him. He'd gone around the pond marrying weeds to weeds and with no Bible to make it stick.

"The love of my life," my mother said. "He was the love of my life, Sam was, and look at me now. Look at both of us now. Or all three, I mean. You, me, and Brad. We don't know bed from bedpost, do we, and we can't help it, can we?"

Brad yanked the stick from my hand and beat at some anthills there and said he never was going to sleep ever again in a bed because beds gave him a sore back. "My back acts up," he said, "and it's all on account of that soft bed. I don't see why we can't sleep on the floor." He'd heard Sam saying that, complaining about soft beds and his poor back, and my mother and I just looked at him whipping the earth with my stick and thinking how much Brad looked like Sam.

"Yes," my mother said, "but I was not about to climb down on the hard floor to sleep with him, and every night, after an hour or so, he'd get up off the floor and climb in beside me. He was willing to endure his sore back for the privilege, is how I thought of it."

We watched Brad beat at the ants scurrying about and did not stop him. We didn't like ants, not these red ants, any better than he did.

"I want ice cream," Brad said, and we both told him to shush or go away and marry something. He poked out his lips about a half-mile but didn't whip my bent stick at us.

"I ought to drain that pond," my mother said. "Drain that whole pond, drain it down to its muck. Somebody was telling me how. But I couldn't bear to see Sam's body in the muck I'd find. I couldn't bear that. Not the love of my life."

"You ought not to talk about it," I said. "It isn't as though you were ever married to him, you know, and it's not your fault you didn't want to sleep every night on a hard floor."

She told me to shush, and Brad crowed to hear that, and jumped up and down with joy for about fifteen minutes.

"I don't know," my mother said. She wiped her eyes and looked off for a long time at the house. "I'd sleep on spikes," she said. "On spikes, now, if he asked me to."

"What's spikes?" Brad said. He'd sleep on them too, he said, and not one of us could do a thing about it.

It was six o'clock in the morning, my mother said, and still dark when Sam got out of bed and put on his clothes. She rolled over, my mother did, and said, "Sam, what in God's name are you doing?"

Sam said he was going down to the pond. He was going down there and this time get a proper reading of the depth, he said. Or die trying.

"I wish he hadn't said that," my mother said. "Not that 'die trying,' because every time I think of it the words just go on ringing in my head. I wish he'd dropped down naked on his pallet beside our bed and pulled me off the mattress down on top of him and kissed me all over, the way some mornings he did. He was a good lover, Sam was, I'll grant him that. But he was fed up, he said, with people asking him how deep that pond was, and the next time they asked it he was going to know the answer and make everyone drop their drawers."

We watched Brad ride about over the weeds on my bent stick like it was a horsie, and I asked him what the name of the horsie was and he said it was named Ice Cream.

"He'd been trying, you see, for weeks," my mother said. "He'd poked and pried with poles and never had hit bottom. Or came close, to know it. He'd dive in and be down for about fifteen minutes and I'd be standing on the shore screaming my head off and hating his guts, or paddling about mad with hysteria in that little boat, then at last he'd pop up shivering and climb into the boat and shrug and say the damn pond had no bottom. It was a goddamn witch's brew down there, and icy-cold, and you couldn't see nothing.

"Well, Christ, Kathleen, you were there. You know it. We've both hollered our heads off a thousand times and wanted to maim his guts, waiting for him to come up.

"So he went out that morning and he was measuring the depth, or trying to, and somehow he drowned. He died." She'd had a feeling that morning, lying in bed, just looking at the ceiling and thinking how it needed painting from all of the smoke – "We smoked so much," she said, "the two of us did, we had to paint every inch of wall and ceiling twice a year, yeah, and throw out the curtains. Just dump a big pile in the yard."

So she'd had that feeling that morning and gone running and there the boat was turned over in the water, one end looped up, and he was nowhere. Well, he was down there.

"So you can marry me to that goddamn pond," she told Brad, "and that will be about as near to having a ring on my finger as I ever got."

"But there is a you-know-what to this story," she said. "You know what? About every two weeks since then I've got a mysterious card from different parts of the world, and it's unsigned, and it could be the son of a bitch isn't at the bottom of that pond after all. It could be. So maybe I'm no nearer that ring than I ever was."

We walked back to the house, both of us holding our skirts high and Brad snaking between first me then her and both of us trying to whack his bottom before he could weasel through.

"You can't!" he sang. "You can't-can't-can't do it!"

He was so happy on that walk and so much a boy you could love we couldn't either one of us wait for him to grow big so we could gobble him up like sugar.

"I don't know," my mother said. "Maybe it's the wages of sin. I've had so many men in my life those cards could be from any one of them. But they did drag the pond and find nothing and I don't know if Sam had decided to leave me and mend his back he wouldn't at least have taken a suit of clothes and whatever money he could have found in my pocketbook."

On our walk back she hugged me and confessed again for the thousandth time her wish that she could tell me who my father was.

"The worst of it," she said, "is that I probably did know once upon a time and it's criminal of me to have forgotten. It's my criminal nature caught up with me now that I'm ancient and sorry, and I wouldn't put it past you to hate me for forgetting which of the sorry ones in my life it was that your daddy was.

"I look at you sometimes and I get the nudge of a memory, just the bare nudge, and then it's gone.

"It could be it was a soldier, as we were saying earlier, because there was a time when soldiers were a dime a dozen and a woman like me could have had my pick from any one of ten thousand. They were going away to be slaughtered, you see, or were just back from the slaughtering, and I didn't see then why the hell not, and the truth is I still don't."

At the house Brad whirled hide-and-seek among the trees and kept calling out each time he showed his face that Sam was his daddy and we could go to blazes if we didn't believe it. Then we went inside and made more lemonade and Brad had his with chocolate ice cream.

"I'm going to keep it all to myself, like a pig," he said, and we both told him that he had the manners of one. Then Brad and I followed my mother upstairs and she opened a dresser drawer. She had about a hundred Gideon Bibles in there picked up from all the hotels and motels she'd ever stayed in, and she told Brad he could take his pick.

He was a long time picking one, them all the same, and the while he was at it she and I stood or jounced on the bed, holding our skirts over our waists and looking at each other's legs in the long mirror.

"He's a cheap one," she said, "whoever he is sending those cards. Probably bone-broke, the way most of them were. If he had any kind of class, it would be roses I'd be getting, though that fits in with Sam since he'd be spending all his money on chiropractors to mend his bad back."

Brad flapped his Bible open and married us to the bed, then went about marrying everything else in the room he could find, including two flies one on top of the other in strenuous – for flies, my mother said – copulation.

My legs were prettier than hers, my mother said, because I had the boy's bottom to go with it, and a Saudi Arabian prince would give a million dollars one day just to peek at my toenails.

Daddy Stump

Bed and I are at the window watching what is going on in there, which is mostly the men in there watching something else, this blue TV light flickering over their faces as they swallow beer and nudge each other, Daddy Stump among them though not nudging anyone himself, as he is hoisted in his usual fatigued manner against the wall, when Bed says, a little too loud, which is how she talks, "Who died in there, Royce? What are we watching, Royce?" Which are good questions, the very both of them good questions that I am having myself, but too loud, attention-grabber questions, so I go to jab my fingers into her eyes to shut her up, when what she is doing is already running, which is the one thing she does first-rate, like Daddy Stump does standing against his walls. That is when the overhead bulb flares in there, inside the room where we are watching through the window what goes on, and a mad scramble from the men in there swarthed under these blue flickers, because the old pig's-head barrel Bed and I are standing on has decided to collapse because of Bed's takeoff footpower when I go to poke her, this poke intended only to shut her up from her speaking of the dead, which she speaks of right and left these days on account of Mama Stump's bedridden plight, like her whole mind these days is consumed with thoughts of how the earth covers you and you down there with your eyes closed and the earth's weight weighing against your closed eyelids, as I do myself these days, when it comes to that.

"Quick, the light!" somebody says in there, first the dive for cover and then somebody says that, one of the former nudgers under the blue flickers, then the next second all of us scrambling, me just catching a glimpse of Bed swooping away around the corner of the house, shouting back, "I told you that old barrel was rotten!" Me in pursuit of her now, since she's running the wrong way, Bed is, into a deadly trap, if you figure the men in there are sharp enough to head for the front door and not the window where we were looking at what was going on in there, and had been since the minute we'd noticed them steering one by one, over the minutes, into that scrungy, run-down, unused place, them furtive and decomposed as something would be furtive burrowing into a hole where, once everyone gets in there, a thing worth looking at might be going on.

But they don't catch us or see us, thank God, maybe because they are too decomposed to swoop outside, or at least too disruptured to exit except by the stealthy departure, just as they'd done one by one in the ingress, their heads slunk down that way, like a chicken will bury hers under wing, since if they swooped out as a gang intent on finding out who it was was sneaking their looks at them they could be identified and hoof-printed, anyone seeing them to ask what they were doing in there, it being condemned property with No Trespassing signs slung all over the yard and trees along with the KEEP OUT's.

Next time they will throw up planks over the window like they ought to have done this time, and you'd think Daddy Stump, snagged up against that wall in that way only he knows how, with a clear shot at what was going on in there, would have thought to do that, him being as well-versed and schooled in spywork and subterfuge – especially since his truck crash – as anyone else in these parts.

But whoa-up.

There is Bed sprawled in a mud puddle at the side of the house, the three black slips she likes to wear all heisted and scrunched up under her elbows, now whimpering a little, not because of the mud but because of the humiliation of having been caught by me for practically the first time since she learned fast running was her excelling point in life.

"Hey, Royce," she says, but I don't wait to see what else is coming out of her mouth, I just snatch her up by her waistbands and bootleg her through the fence hedge, and back home fast as we can fly.

So we can be there, in the front room with the TV turned up loud, vibrating the little glass shoes it sits on so as not to scar the floor, Bed down on the floor spread out on the dog's old newspapers, to save the mat, which for unknown reasons is prized around here, and me sitting eel-bent on the fold-out smelly couch with my hands up over my face, honing rapt-eyed on that TV set, when Daddy Stump hobbles in. Like if I bat my eyes the whole show and the crate holds it will plain disappear. Like if you don't concentrate fully on every second of your life then the whole ceiling, to instance one thing that will, will collapse.

When Daddy Stump comes in. This being about three minutes, or pretty soon anyway, after we have fled from watching what was going on inside that house with him shagged up against the wall, which is where he goes now, to his usual wall, his head at the very same grease spot, after first turning down the TV to a whisper you can't hear even if you crouch inside the thing.

"You kids look a tad out of breath," he says.

"You kids look," he says, in his own whisper that you have to strain to make out or know he's talking at all, "like you been up to something you shouldna' been up to," he says. His voice rising now and getting more meanness into it, the tone getting more his own now, like the words have to gnaw up past his wired teeth. This for some reason making me relax a bit, though not much. Not for long. Because how he finishes his speech is with, "And maybe I'm going to have to strap you, both of you, give you a few knobs to think about. The thing is, which first?"

So he's slipping his belt out of his pants as he says this, in no hurry to get down to it, this slow way meaning he means business now, which I see with just the half of my eyes, just up to that belt and no more, just up to that buckle, for instance, where there's a dab of red that could be old bloodstains, mine or Bed's or his own leaking out. Bed no doubt glomming onto the same, though otherwise we have the usable half of our eyes glued at these whispering people on the TV set, like they are watching us and being careful to keep their voices low so as not to intrude or halt anything going on in here, and whose watching and silent talking make me think of the last time he had that strap snapping his business, when the people across the road called the law, which is what got the dog started, the law's arrival, and ended up with Daddy Stump's disfigurement, if disfigured is how you'd describe the condition he's got himself in now, which I wouldn't, not to his face, and Bed wouldn't either, despite a natural talent inclining her to spit it out. That head of his still swathed in the white bandages, though them not white now, from the surgeon's brainwork.

"I think it was I told you to stay home," Daddy Stump says with these teeth.

Then he has this clump of my hair in his hand, twisting, while I squint my eyes tight, my breath flat, catching the odd wet blink of Bed down on the floor with her hand crawling up under the black slips to scratch at where chunks of mud are drying in jigsaw shapes on her behind because the heat in this house is up to a constant 85° because of the infirmed one's shivery condition in the Fatal Care Unit.

I get an "ouch" or two out, hardly anything else including my breath, as meanwhile Daddy Stump is pulling out my hair until he can decide which body part will be juiciest to his strap as he goes about finding out whether we know or don't know what it was he and his buddyroles were watching in there in that KEEP OUT house down the road, under their blue flickers, or whether we've been here the whole of the day glued to his dumb TV box, which is how with not one spoken word the world can hear what's going on in here.

Which is a good thing, too, because what we hear in the absence is the tick of the kitchen clock, the bong-bong recitation of minute and hour. Which reminds us and Daddy Stump, too, that it is time for the nursing rounds, time to turn Mama Stump on her sheets in there in the Coma Room in her bedridden, no-holds-barred, write-off condition.

"You two Joes just hold on," says Daddy Stump, giving a hard belt-lash to my ankle bones as he hobbles off in that up-down, swaying way he hobbles since his truck crash.

"Perfection!" Bed says, "Utter perfection!"

Yelling this out, along with a big grin which comes out at the same time, which statement I guess is occasioned by the new delightful sensation she's feeling from all this mud drying on her, even those clumps lumped in her behind, which would worry me.

I crawl up and flip the TV channel, wondering what another place would look like when you can't hear anyone saying anything though the lips are moving like they think you ought to be able to. "You stay off that mat," I tell Bed, because I see her inching that way for the comfort, like she's decided the newspaper is something you'd put down for the dog to do his stuff on, that being how we did it around here before the dog ended up on Daddy Stump's truck hood and came through the windshield into his lap, where she still wouldn't quit, all while he's revving the truck to shoot it by those law officers who have squared off their Plymouth up by the mailbox, and squared off themselves behind it, their holster belts up near their titties, those blue lights whipping.

Daddy Stump, in his truck that time, sees this.

He views it and is considering the choices even as the dog comes through the windshield. He's got to career off the rear-end of that Plymouth, hit the ditch and take out the mailbox, take out a few scrub trees and part of the fence, if he's to make it. Which he likely would have but for the pistol shot and the dog which is up on his chest now in a blur of broken glass slobbering her licks over his face, her legs doing a jujitsu over the steering wheel, so happy that this time that dog is getting to go with Daddy Stump where it is that dog thinks he is going.

"Oh Swami," Bed says to me when, with these raw welts on her legs, which I guess is why she's taken to wearing Mama Stump's black slips that Mama Stump won't ever recall once wearing herself. Those people on the TV go right on with their mute talking.

A bit later I hear the door open in the Intensive Care Room down the hall where Mama Stump abides the hour.

"Water," Daddy Stump calls.

Which Bed purses her lips at, watching me to see if we

have heard any words hailing our way from the Death Chamber.

A minute later the door rattles open again, him saying, "Didn't I tell you to bring your mama a glass of water?"

Bed grins, like she's saying she never heard of water and wouldn't know where to look for it in its pure form.

"And I mean now," Daddy says, while I hold my breath to see will be add, "And I don't mean maybe," or will it be, "I don't mean tomorrow."

But he just bangs shut the door.

Bed is now clumping stiff-limbed around the room, looking to see will her mud suit fall off or will she be able to wear it forever.

"Stay away from that mat," I tell her again, for that mat's precious and could be is all that's left from the Stump twosome's old bridal suite.

Bed clumps behind me to the kitchen, where I draw the water. She's saying, "Mama Stump gets out of that bed when no one's here." She's saying, "I've seen Mama Stump's footprints."

"Where?" I say, watching the water run over the glass and over my hand and dribble down my arm to the floor, so that pretty soon there's a puddle there Bed can squish her toes about in. "On the linoleum?" I say. "Where have you seen the stalker's footprints?"

"All over," Bed says. "Mostly on the ceiling."

"Hip-hip, hooray," she says.

She points up at the ceiling where the light bulb is hanging from the chawed-up, fly-speck cord, which reminds me of the dozen or so light bulb spares we've now got somewhere in the house, from the time this woman came to the door wearing push-pedal leggings and with this lopsided face, selling "Electric light bulbs," she said, "of assorted wattage."

"Proceeds to charity," she said, to Daddy Stump who is there by the front door holding her at bay, saying, "That's us."

Bed says, "Excellent," watching the puddle spread out towards her feet which she steps back from, not ready yet to squish about and upset the status quo of her mud suit. "Excellent, excellent," she says, raising her black slips up over her waist and on up till the three black slips are over her head, maybe in the darkness of that headspace remembering what I am remembering myself, which is Daddy Stump at the front door talking to this woman selling electric light bulbs of assorted wattage and telling her that he will bet her a dollar he can illuminate any one of these light bulbs she's holding without even screwing that bulb into a socket of any kind but simply by putting that light bulb screw-end into his mouth. And the woman saying, "I never heard of that," but not saying she will bet, though Bed and I are searching everywhere we can think to find that dollar. Because if Daddy Stump can do what he claims he can do, and do it without any tricks, then he is a man mankind has been underestimating all these years.

A minute later, he's doing it. He's doing it without even the dollar. He screws the light bulb between his lips, screws it tight, standing there at the front door looking out at the dark night and the lopsided woman's face with her open mouth. He does it, nothing happens, then he crouches, grimaces, and gives that bulb a last extra twist. The light flickers, it goes out.

"Uh-oh, pay up," Bed and I say, because Daddy Stump hasn't said anything about flickers. But he smiles. He gives that bulb a thump, and that light comes on. It comes on and stays on. About forty wattage on, I'd say. It doesn't flicker any more, even as he says "Excuse me, Sweetheart," a rumble, but that's what it sounds like, and he strolls past the light woman and down the steps into the yard, where he performs these several little spins, these struts, his head cocked, like he wants us to observe that he is not attached to by wires or On and Off switches of any kind, except maybe his tongue.

Because later he tells us the tongue does it, gets the job done, but only if he's been drinking, which he was doing that night, running back and forth from the Intensive Care Chamber where Mama Stump presides in her agony, to his hooch stash behind the cornmeal.

So I am now bringing in the glass of water which he has called for and which he cannot get himself, the water that is meant for Mama Stump who is too infirmed to drink it or even to know her nurse has come with it. Daddy Stump is heisted up the wall where I expect him to be, near the head of Mama Stump's bed, and she is there laid out in bed with only her dark brow and her closed eyes showing, the skin of those eyes dark as pecan shell, these peach-pit eyes which are always closed, not even breathing insofar as I or Bed can tell, though Daddy Stump claims she can hear and understand every word said, or others unsaid, so watch it, he says, if you don't want to get swatted.

But he does not say that now. What he is saying now, which is like he's inside a story he has been telling Mama Stump over the past minutes, is "Itu, itu."

This with a kind of smirk, or laugh, on his face, the same as was when he was doing his forty watts with the lopsided woman's light bulb. All around the four walls are these head-high grease spots in the past coma year he's put there. He is heisted up against the wall, the leg cast, which is all the way up to his fanny, covered by his supertwill ratty-edged trousers, only his pink toes with the long toenails showing, his head scrunched down deep into his shoulder blades or collarbone, deep into the grimy, yellowish neck-brace. That one rebuilt shoulder riding up even with his turbaned ears. This lick of black shiny sideburn hair, which he wouldn't let them shave when they were scraping his head down to the hide, poking out from the wrappings wild as a crow's nest.

"Itu," he's saying. "Itu."

Laughing full-out now, and looking down at Mama Stump like he's sure she's laughing too, if only under the covers where no one will ever see it.

I lift out Mama Stump's hand, her arm brown as ginger, like a dead, shriveled root you'd pull from the ground, and I wrap her cold fingers around the glass, though she'll never know it and pretty soon the glass will plop over and wet the bed, the same as Bed will me once we are sawing the logs on that open-out couch.

It's the asbestos, according to Daddy Stump. The asbestos in the walls, which has brought about this strange discoloration of the loved one's skin, and he will sue the pants off somebody, once he figures out who.

"Itu, I'm going," he's saying. "They've got this scrawl down at the bottom of the screen," he's telling the patient. "This white print scrawl which is a translation of what these Japanese characters are saying up in the working part. The picture's working part, where this little fellow is working all-out, on the top of this nice-looking woman. They been going at it, you see, and when he gets there, does he say, I'm coming? The way me and you would? No, what he's saying is 'Itu, itu,' with this thrashing of breath, these grunts, with this white scrawl down at the bottom telling us what he's really saying is 'I'm going, I'm going!'"

"Itu, itu!"

He even comes down from the wall, Daddy Stump does, to slap his knee, his casted leg, he's enjoying his story that much, and now looking over at Mama Stump under her covers to see if she's got it yet, is she laughing yet, which she isn't and won't.

"That's what they say over there," he tells her.

"What do you think of that?"

But Mama Stump doesn't care what they say over there, or over here, or anywhere else in the world. Mama Stump's gone to where she can't think about it.

So I leave her fingers wrapped around that glass, and slip on out, glad for the minute that I have not had to brush her teeth or wash her limbs, coax the pudding cleanser into her hair, salve her, spray her, switch her backside over to the cooler portion of sheet – do anything other than get that water – as he slumps back to the wall and goes on with that "Itu" business, or wherever it is he goes when he goes in there to tell her what it is he goes in there to tell her.

In the kitchen, Bed is splashing up water from the floor pool, all over herself, wetting down that mud, which she's got slung now from one end to the other, over the dirty dishes, the curtains, the windows and door, and chunks of it up on the ceiling and on that hanging light bulb.

"Stupendous," is what she's saying.

"First-rate."

"Incredibly Yours."

Now it's night. It is night, and bedtime, and Bed is getting ready for bed. Getting Bed ready for bed is what brings on my shivers, for to get Bed ready I have first to open the couch, check the wet spots, root out the pillows, see the rubber sheet is stretched flat, see she has her stuffed doll, raise the windows and fluff the sheets and spread the towels over the wet spots. I have to get her promise that tonight she won't.

"Oh no, Oh Swami. Never again."

I have first to do with her as Mama Stump has said she once had to do with me. I have to sit her down on the potty, to seat her there and coax her, shake her, run water from the taps, from the taps and the coffin-box shower stall, and sing her ditties about little girls on leaking boats in the tranquil flow of rivers, and press and poke her kidneys, pour glasses of water down between her legs, into her crev-ices, and woo her, browbeat her, though in the end, whether she tinkles or doesn't tinkle it will come to the same thing: in the night I will feel her cold puddle, I will come awake to the feel of its icy widening, her puddle spreading, arriving on under us and around us in a circle wide as your backside will ever find you, then to hear Bed murmuring, "Excellent, excellent," as she drops back into sleep again, her hand still and soft in mine, just the way Mama Stump said mine was in hers in those days long ago, before we had a dog, or asbestos, or Bed, or a house that had, as Daddy Stump likes to say, walls we could call our own.

Mama Stump is beside me on one side and Daddy Stump is guiding me on the other, scurrying me down the hall, both of them shouting "Hold it, hold it, one more second now," Mama Stump with this while towel spun over her head and in her soft black slip, her red toenails, Daddy Stump with his hairy legs, and me with my little pecker poked way out, holding it, us scooting along. Until it starts whipping about like a running hose you can't catch hold of, it snaking each which way, on their dancing feet and over their legs, splattering the walls, as they whip me and my little thing over the toilet where maybe one last little spurt will spurt down.

Then back to the bed, though not my bed, in between them there in their big dry bed, Daddy Stump's hips about where my feet are, me leaning into his mattress weight as Mama Stump collects my hand over her warm belly and laces both of her hands into mine, then his hand there too, and Daddy Stump complaining, "He won't never grow out of it," while Mama Stump sighs, they both sigh, and she answers back, "This is nice, so nice. So let's hush, let's all of us Stumps hush and go to sleep now."

Cornfields

Dodie, my owner, is walking through the cornfield. She wanted me to walk with her, but I am over in the potato patch, hoe in hand.

Potato sprouts are tender to the touch. Frankly, I think it would be fine to eat the leaves and stems, they look delicious, but Dodie says, Fat chance, you'd die or get sick, which would be worse, and then where'd I be?

In many places in the world I'm sure they eat the air part of the potato plant and if I were in those places I would. But in this part of the world we are more or less blessed, and I do what I'm told.

"Can you see me?" Dodie shouts.

Of course I can see her, as easily as she can see me.

I know what is on her mind. We planted the field, and planted it close to the house, just so we could. She's always wanted to, she says.

But the corn isn't high enough. Another month.

In some parts of the world the corn will be already high enough and people, no doubt, are hidden in the rows this very minute, doing what Dodie wants to do.

Last year it was string beans, in the string beans.

Dodie talks a good deal about having been an only child. Sometimes that's something special and at other times she hates it. She wishes her parents had lived to see her in this house, on this land, with the mortgage all but paid off and an actual drawbridge she's had me build over the creek.

They'd like you, she says.

They'd approve.

They'd like you, she says, or you'd have to ship out.

The drawbridge she had me build will of course keep no one out, since "the enemy," as Dodie calls them, could wade the creek, they could even jump it in spots, or stride a dry bottom in the hot season, but the idea appeals to her.

She's got pictures of her parents all over, from childhood on to the grave.

We've got pictures of us too, though they only start last year with the string beans, when the string beans were teensy things. There are pictures of Dodie driving in the posts, and pictures of her unwinding and tying off the string, and there are pictures of us practically naked between the rows, though there is no picture of us together.

That's a picture we carry in our minds, she says.

We are intertwined between the rows, she says, and in her mind the rows go on forever. The rows outlast eternity, she says, and we, there between the rows, we outlast it too.

That is how she talks sometimes, and, myself, I like it. I like it that she has been talking that way about the corn since it sprouted. The corn will be more fun than the string beans, she says, because corn is more "opulent." It is more "opulent" and thus more private.

I say, "Dodie, if we can outlast eternity in rows of string beans, then how can corn beat that?"

She says, "You don't understand anything, do you?" She says, "I am talking about the 'refining of quality' in our lives. I am talking about the establishment of new definitions here."

She wants little gates installed at both sides of the

drawbridge, and yesterday she pointed out the new lumber and the nails and told me to get to it.

I said, "Dodie, it's on the 'chores' list right where you put it, just after 'dig new well.'"

She says, "I know it, but here is a verity: You have an inclination to dawdle."

Yet she dances now between the corn rows while I am the one here in the potato patch attending to the weeding.

She is supposed to be there with a hose, attending to the watering.

Here is a verity of my own: We look happier than her parents did. We look happier in our photos than her parents do in theirs.

They look a sad lot, in those pictures. Haunted is how they look to me, and in not one are they smiling.

I see Dodie sometimes lifting those pictures, studying them, pretending to dust or wipe them, and I know she is thinking the same thing herself.

Her parents are buried on a rise behind the house. She had their bodies dug up, got permission somehow – on account of her mental well-being, or so I've heard.

On account of its being necessary to her well-being.

I don't know how she managed this.

I don't imagine securing permission to dig up dead bodies for reburial in another place is an easy feat.

In this part of the world, in this rural part where we live, I do not even know who one would approach.

In some parts of the world, of course, this practice might be quite customary.

I am intrigued that the deed was allowed on account of its being necessary to Dodie's well-being. It intrigues me to ponder what her mental state was at that time, and what dejection and fatigue she might now feel had their uprooting not come to pass.

"I wanted it done for a long time," she says, "and now I've got mental peace."

I too have more mental peace now than I once did, of that I am absolutely certain.

Dodie sees me looking at her, sees me observing her, and she will say, "Yeah, you love me, but I'm not the end of the world. Love isn't either," she says.

"I might release you from your servitude," she says, "might let you have the freedom of the ballot and the rights and claims normal people have, if ever you stopped looking at me with those goofy eyes."

I say, "Dodie, you haven't heard me complaining, have you? You haven't heard me asking for the ballot, have you?"

"See that you don't," she says.

I have expressed a few concerns: I've suggested we get a dog, or at least chickens, but Dodie says nothing doing.

Dodie says a horse would be fine, nothing wrong with a horse. But it takes a lot to feed a horse, to keep a horse happy, she says, and she will mull it over.

The corn is only about up to her knees.

"Look at me!" she says.

She had on this red halter a minute ago, now that's gone.

The first thing she did once she had her parents under the ground again was to buy these two red kerosene lanterns. You can look out the windows at night, through the night, and see the flickering.

My job in the morning is to go and blow out the lanterns and see soot doesn't cover the globes.

My job is to see the lanterns have a steady supply of kerosene.

That, and plant the corn, the potatoes, and last year the string beans.

I call them "running" beans, but Dodie says that's wrong, they are "climbing" beans or "string" beans because of the strings we run up between stakes to grow them on.

It's best to avoid arguments with her.

The potatoes are "new" potatoes, which is how she likes them, and she has me dig them up before they can get big and brown and the kind of potato you'd like to bake.

"Don't ask so many questions," she tells me, so I don't.

But I wonder about the state of her "well-being" before I entered the picture.

Her mother was seventy-eight years old when she died.

Her father was seventy-seven.

I know that because it said so on the stone.

Dodie didn't want the stone moved. It's still at their old grave, I guess, waiting for another pair that has their same names and died the same ages, the same year.

That's what Dodie says. It doesn't make any sense to me, except in a roundabout way that I get glimmers of now and then.

They died together, in a car crash, I figure, though Dodie never speaks of this.

She never says how they died. She picks up their photographs, she dusts them, she moves them from one spot to another, but what I've noticed is that those she attends to most frequently are those in which the two are together.

Yesterday I discovered she uses dye on her hair and it's a burnt-sienna color which gets on her fingers because she won't wear the little plastic gloves. To tell the truth, it gets all over her, on her stomach and legs, little finger marks, so I don't know how she thought she could keep it a secret or why she wanted to.

I get a feeling sometimes, especially in the mornings when I'm blowing out their lanterns, that the people buried out back are not her true parents, but Dodie tells me to shut my mouth.

I get the feeling, looking at their pictures, that they are too old to have a daughter Dodie's age.

"If you care about my mental well-being," she says, "or if you have any decency left, you'll just keep quiet about things that you could not possibly understand."

It strikes me that among all those pictures there ought to be at least one of Dodie with her parents.

But I am not brave enough, or dumb enough, to inquire about this.

Mine is a subservient role around here; it's taken me a while, but I've learned precisely how long my leash is.

She likes for me to wash her back, wash it in this claw-footed bathtub set up at the back of the house, with a little hose we can run through the window and attach to the kitchen faucet.

"Now scrub hard," she says.

She stares at their graves the whole time, and wants me to put up a wrought-iron fence with a fancy little iron gate we will have to pass through.

I say to her, Dodie, there ought to be a marker of some kind back there, something to identify them, and she says, "Who is running this show?" She says, "I know who they are."

I say, Dodie, what were they like, your parents? and she snaps her eyes shut. "They were *nice* people," she says in a mean voice, and then she streaks inside and slams the door.

On other days she says to me, "Where are your parents buried?" And I say, "Dodie, they are not buried anywhere yet."

I've told her that a thousand times, but she always seems to forget.

I say to her, "Dodie," I say, "I don't know where around here I could go to buy wrought-iron fencing."

She says, "There's that old abandoned church not far

from here. We could steal the fencing from the graveyard behind that church."

I have a feeling sometimes that Dodie does not mean to let the dead have their rest. I have the feeling that she and I have different ideas about death.

She says, "For that matter, we could steal all the wrought-iron fencing at that site and erect it around the whole of this house."

I say, "Dodie, I am not a thief."

She says, "I own you, and you are whatever I say you are."

It is best not to argue with her. Perhaps some place in this world there is someone who would, though I have strong doubts.

I've searched in her cupboards and bins, in her dresser drawers, I've rooted through boxes in the basement, but I've yet to find a single picture of Dodie with her parents. There are pictures of Dodie little, of Dodie growing up, but in these pictures she's always alone, and the background, what you see in the background, doesn't look like any place around here.

It looks like a place in another part of the world.

And in those pictures of her parents what you can make out in the background doesn't faintly resemble that background you see in Dodie's pictures.

I figure Dodie went to a stranger's house and stole – bought or stole – every picture of these two she could find.

I figure this is the kind of behavior she was capable of back there when she was in her troubled state.

"Get to work!" she calls to me now.

She's pulled up the water hose and she's standing there now, between the rows, spraying the corn.

She's half-naked and waving that red halter.

It rained this morning, a brief, hard rain, but she's spraying the corn anyhow.

"I give it two weeks," she tells me.

I give it a month, though I will not argue with her.

It's got to be full-grown, she's already told me that.

We don't really need a new well, but Dodie says it is best to be on the safe side.

The corn Dodie is standing in is supposed to be a fast-growth variety, but Dodie had the idea it was going to shoot up overnight.

She was in a pout about that most of the past evening.

She said to me yesterday, "We've all known panic. We've all had spears in our chests. You have yourself, or how otherwise could you have let yourself be sold as a slave?"

I said, Dodie, it isn't something you *let* happen.

Sometimes she will leave her bed in the night and I will see her out striding the corn rows with her flashlight.

You will see her down on her knees having little chats with this and that stalk.

What I say is that the corn is faster than the string beans were last year.

What I say is that there are any number of weeping willows around this place and we could lose ourselves under those willows the same as we could in that corn.

And who is to know or object anyhow?

"I wouldn't be caught dead doing it under no tree," is what she says.

"There's high grass," I say.

What she says is she's not rolling in high grass the way a dumb animal would.

The barn needs cleaning out, she says, it needs new hay in the hayloft. She wouldn't altogether discount the hayloft as a location for "our earthly pleasures," as she calls them.

What I say is the bedroom has served the purpose for a good number of people a good number of years and why is it she thinks nothing will work unless you have these strange ideas?

"You can leave any time you want to," is what she says. "I'll sign you your freedom notice in a flash, the minute you let me know you want it."

She can be rude, or talk hard sometimes, but I don't feel I've got any real complaint.

I get three squares a day and I've got a roof over my head.

Having the ballot would only give me trouble I don't want.

It's going to be nice in that corn.

We've been watering it daily, morning and evening, speeding it along.

Sometimes when I'm going out to tend the two graves, some mornings, she will say, "Tell my parents how I'm doing. Tell them how happy I am. Tell them I've found my mental peace."

"Tell them the enemy can't get in here."

"Tell them to rest easy, that we are out of harm's way, here."

Which I do. I tell it to them on mornings when I'm standing out there in the dew in my bare feet, blowing out the wicks and refilling their lanterns with kerosene.

"She's happier than you two ever were," is what I tell them.

I wait for them to say something back, but they've kept quiet up to now.

I can't say I really know how happy she is, though most of the time she appears to be.

When I was washing her back this morning she said she was feeling blue. She said she was feeling like a blue Monday all over, and I ought to get in the tub with her and cheer her up. I ought to, she said, but it just felt so good having me behind her scrubbing her back the way only I could.

I said, "Dodie, why are you blue?" but she didn't answer me. A minute later she splashed up out of the water and went whizzing around the house to dry herself off.

In summer, she won't ever let me use a towel.

She's gone now. The hose is spraying the corn, she's rigged it up there on a high, pronged stick, but where she has got to I don't know.

The air is heavier down here. I can feel it on my face, the spray from that hose. A fine mist covers the field and it seems to be lifting and spreading. When I squint, it seems to go on forever, just as those corn rows do. Just as the string beans did.

There may be somewhere in this world another place just like this place. I wouldn't want to claim it was impossible.

I don't know where Dodie has got to. She disappears sometimes for long intervals, doesn't return for hours. For days, sometimes, though those are not times I like to think about.

There's her red halter, hanging from corn.

There's her little what-she-calls hot pants.

So she's naked, wherever she is.

We had hard rain this morning, the earth is wet, is soggy, and I could follow her footsteps down the rows, follow them to wherever it is she is going, was there any point in it.

Maybe to high grass.

Or I could wait. I could dig up these new potatoes, get them to the table.

Put in a few fine touches on that drawbridge.

Consider that wrought-iron business.

Do a little divining for the new well.

All in all, that's probably the better idea.

Pretty Pictures

Tここ here are pretty pictures and not-so-pretty pictures.
You know that. We would probably agree which is
which. There is the not-so-pretty picture of my wife kissing another man. But that's looking at it from my side.
From her side it is no doubt a very pretty picture. We know
how it feels, don't we, to kiss someone we are attracted to,
illicit or otherwise. The picture isn't the same, illicit, but
the feeling is. You go up on your toes with a feeling like
that. You kiss, and you go up on your toes, illicit or otherwise; you go off into orbit. That's what the kissing does,
and maybe the prettiness or the not-so-prettiness of the
moment is somehow beside the point, and ought to be,
somehow, not a thing that we dwell upon.

We've all been deprived of too many kisses and that is one
reason we do it. Let's say that is one reason. There are other
reasons, of course, but let's not dwell upon it.

I did not set out to tell you about my wife kissing another
man. It was not a picture, at the start, I even had in mind
telling you. It was an ugly picture, to my mind, which just
jumped in. It got in front and momentarily dislodged the
pretty picture I was contemplating telling you about.

Here it is, that pretty picture. My father and I are passing
along the street and the sights I see seem very strange and

unfamiliar to me. All the angles are screwy; they are screwy and cockeyed. People look short, very short, and dogs and cats are practically foreign creatures, so small are they in their appearance. Children, other children, they are the smallest beings yet. You can look over fences you've never looked over before. You can see into certain windows, into houses, you've never looked into before.

It comes to me, in this picture, that I am riding my father's shoulders. That is where I am, up there on his shoulders, my legs around his neck, his hands gripping my ankles, my head above his head. My chin, at times, rests in his hair. I am laughing, I am at times waving my arms, so fond I am of being up there. I am delighted with this view of the world.

That is the pretty part. Here is the not-so-pretty part. We go through a doorway, and we both crouch. I do not know which doorway it is. Maybe we have circled the block and returned home and that is the doorway we are entering. The picture dissolves at this point. I know we are passing through a door, but what awaits us inside is not a picture I can see. It is not even out-of-focus, that picture. It is blank; it does not exist.

Here is an even prettier picture, a picture prettier than the first part of that picture was. I am again riding my father's shoulders. We are out on the street once again, but here is why this picture is prettier. I am eating an ice-cream cone. I am smiling, eating that cone. My father is also eating an ice-cream cone and he too is smiling. I have two scoops on mine, one chocolate and one vanilla, with the chocolate on top, and have just begun my licks. I have an entire double-scoop cone to look forward to. My father has a single cone, vanilla, I think, and he has not yet touched his. One of his hands grips my ankle. I have my free hand across his brow, to hold on, and sometimes I jiggle and that hand slides down to cover his eyes. He walks with one foot in the gutter, the other on the sidewalk, and up on his shoulders I weave from side to side. He says, How do you like your ice cream? and I say, How do you like yours? And we laugh, as though we have said the funniest thing in the world.

The ice cream melts and oozes over my fingers and it drops into his hair. It's a hot day, he says. Where do you want to go now?

Here that picture becomes not-so-pretty, what little there is of it, because I don't know where I want to go now. I want the ride to start back over; I want him to lift me to his shoulders, to hold my ankle, to walk again to wherever it was we bought that ice cream. I want him to walk on and off the curb as he has done, I want to slip and slide up there, and for my ice cream to drip into his hair. When he asks, Where do you want to go next? already that picture is closing down, the picture is dissolving, and a second later I will no longer be riding on his shoulders. The picture will vanish and I will not know where I have gone next.

This is what I felt when I saw my wife kissing another man. It is what I felt when I saw her coming out of his bedroom. I did not know where my world had gone or if I had a place within it. The door to that bedroom rattled as it closed, which was precisely what I felt inside, that rattling, and I could not say what was beyond that door or any other door. I think what I felt was that she had left her love behind that closed door and the only picture I had left was of that closed door.

So that is the picture I have now, of that door, and it is the only picture. It is the picture which keeps jumping in; it dislodges all other pictures. It is not a pretty picture, from my point of view, and I do not know what to do with it. I do not know where I can go next. It will not dissolve, that picture won't, and it will go with me wherever it is I choose, or don't choose, to go.

The door is not a part of her picture. Her picture is composed only of whatever it was that went on while she was inside. She has that picture, of what went on inside, and the next picture, as she closed the door, of my stunned face. The man inside the room, the man she kissed, he has his pictures too. I expect my father, for that matter, has his own pictures and that these do not include his riding his son upon his shoulders or of their eating ice cream and the ice cream dripping into his hair. It is a fact that I never in real life rode his shoulders, or even saw him once I had reached the age of two. Possibly he rode another kid on his shoulders; more likely, he didn't. I have never imagined that children were a part of this earth that my father cared for.

So the picture I have of me riding my father's shoulders is one born out of the rides I have given my own child, together with those sights I have witnessed of other men and women riding their sons and daughters. It is the picture I had in mind to tell you when I began telling you this, before I saw her kissing him and that door closing, because this, her kissing him and emerging from his bedroom and that door rattling shut with its full awful power, is not a picture I would, in the normal course of events, have mentioned. It is the one true picture, the one picture drawn from real life, but it is not a picture that will do any of us any good.

Mama Tuddi Tried

Mama Tuddi in the jury box can't get her eyes focused. She's got these half-glasses, magnifiers they're called, $8.95 at the Walgren's, and they sit on her nose like bags of see-through lint. She can see her hands, she can see her jury mates one to each side, though the rest is a fuzz. She keeps wiping, wiping. Her regular glasses for long range, tinted two colors, dark and darker, have a break in the lens and she won't be putting these on, only when she gets home to her own four walls will she be putting these on. A woman have her pride, she have her poise and cool to think of.

This woman on her right have a pretty nice pair, not too tacky. She have a false hairpiece in her own hair, though; that bring her down some in Mama Tuddi's estimation. She have a sweet suit on. If Mama Tuddi had the shape that suit would be on her own self, with a little bright scarf to tie at the throat. The woman is the fidgety, nervous type so it don't matter what clothes she wear, it all going to waste on that frame like tar in a bucket. She have her body leaning away from Mama Tuddi. Lot of hand-clenching and foot-turning going on over there.

Mama Tuddi lean that same way herself. The man to her left have a mean smell. He a big fat man in a shiny suit, the sleeves most up to his elbows. Down at his shoes she can see through the fuzz his white ankle bones. What the color remind her of is chicken skin in the A&P. You git that chicken home, you throw it in the pan and brown it up, but before it browned that chicken skin is the ugliest white meat you ever see. Other than that, she got nothing against chicken, nor a white man either.

She got nothing against this one sitting in the dock, come to that.

She done catched him snitching a look at her, at her especially, and while he resemble a man would commit a crime, still to her mind they have to prove it first. He white, he pudgy, you could stash two suitcases in his jaws, but she ain't going to be no party to no railroading gang.

They don't like it, they can get theirselves another gal. She ain't ask for this gig in the first place.

Mama Tuddi lean a little more, for this fat man to her right getting riper by the minute. He have skinny ankles for a fat man. He have big scuff shoes which to his credit he have tried to put a buff on. The smell, it seem, is under his arm, for he have a wide sweat spot there. He is the fidgety type too. He like to poke Mama Tuddi with his two-ton shoulder every chance he git.

Heart attack country over there, Mama Tuddi thinks. I gave him maybe a year.

He the kind of man you can hear breathe, which disrupt your own breath and make you fidget yourself.

Some fool behind her she can feel breathing on her neck.

These lawyers been going at it all day, you'd think the criminal had robbed a bank.

Kleenex time again. What she have spent on Kleenex this week she could OWN a bank.

Wouldn't you know it, her change fall out.

Someone giggle across the room, maybe the criminal

himself. Mama Tuddi hope so, for in her mind a man ain't ready for the scrap heap so long as he can see the mirth in things.

Mama Tuddi wish she could a minute borrow the glasses of the suit-woman on her right. She want to git herself a nice sharp look at the other people in this jury box. She want to inquire can she git herself another seat, and she want to ask can she go over and look the criminal in the eye, for one look to her mind would settle the case. Unless he a dope-runner and can't look at her without hanging his head or his britches falling down, then she reckon he innocent as the next man. He stout, she can see that even with the fuzz, but stoutness so far as she knows ain't yet no crime. She a bit stout herself, now that she on the roast beef track.

But she shedding it one of these days.

The man up behind what she have heard called the bench, he a half hippopotamus himself. That a funny name to call it, a bench, to Mama Tuddi's way of thinking. If all you have is a bench then you can't expect to have much sitting behind it, that is how she see it.

Not that it ain't some gown he have on. She have seen another twelve just like it every week in her church choir.

She wonder when she and her other jury crew going to git a chance to go to the bathroom.

It way past smoke time too.

She certainly wish the pace pick up a bit. She sit here long enough she wonder if finally someone will think to pass coffee and a biscuit around. Nobody these days give a thought to a person's needs: that is the trouble with this world.

Mama Tuddi wish for one day she could run the show. She do the job right. She would, and she know a lot of people feel the same way. They do a bum job, even these people wanting a change, but the fact they think it prove her point; nobody satisfied. You want satisfaction, you give Mama Tuddi the reins.

That is the issue ought to be brought before this court, not no petty crime the criminal likely didn't do in the first place. Far as she know, the hangman ain't yet said the condemned hurt no one. He ain't taken no knife to no poor girl's throat. He had, and she knew it, she'd hang him herself.

The spectators sparse. That a good sign to Mama Tuddi this judge do not know how to run a good show. Her own show, The Mama Tuddi Show, is by now pretty much a household word. She have a hundred people each night clamoring for studio space. She going syndicated one of these days. She going to put in a religious hour, git herself a pastor to sit on the sideline, give a friendly blessing or quick healing job while she do the hard part. Once that happen her show going to go through the roof. The network people going to be chasing her tail. What she need now is a new sponsor knows where the bacon is. The Double Ola people big, they plenty big, but they not big enough. They got to go some before they throw Pepsi off the rack.

Sunbonnet Foods, they dickering with her.

Maybe she go with Sunbonnet, maybe she will, it have a long life on the shelf. They pack a thick goose, the Sunbonnet Foods.

Mama Tuddi remove her glasses from her nose. Nothing happening in this burg she can't miss.

She think again about that woman on her right. It a sex smell that woman have. It all over her A to Z. You have that smell, you can't leave it home, Mama Tuddi knows that from her own experience with men. It is why they always buttering you up, sliding around your feet, always chomping at your ear, putting their hands where even a bear wouldn't have nerve to go. Oh yes, if there is one thing Mama Tuddi knows it is the zoo. She know one man love her so much he take out an insurance policy on her life. "The sight of you keeps me kicking," he say. "I lose you I've good as lost the race."

Of course, he never have her to begin with, that the funny part. When it come to certain men Mama Tuddi take the arm's length approach.

The line ever changing, but it been a coon's age since she not have a line.

That LeRoy, he the one party to slip out of the noose. Many the nights now, by her lonesome, coming home from her taping or out on the roast beef circuit, she wonder whatever happen to him. Have he got hogtied, and if so who the lucky gal? She still roll over in her bed in the weary a.m. pining for the phone to ring.

"That you, LeRoy? It four a.m. by the pussycat's howl but you come on over, there ain't a minute Mama Tuddi ain't on the job."

She sound tacky to her own self sometimes when she talking to LeRoy in her own private mind.

She find herself coming into the lonely hotel room these days, that little red telephone light is blinking, LeRoy is the first name leap to her head. "He trying to git through," is what she say. "He doing his level best."

But it been a long time now. It the good ones always gitting away.

Not that she don't know LeRoy's trouble. One woman never going to be enough for him. He need four or five just to soak up the extra charm he have.

It a pity, is what it is.

He good as lick you up and down everytime you think of him.

Mama Tuddi wonder if this woman on her right have a man like LeRoy on her case. Maybe that's why she got the fidgets, can't wait to git back to him.

She hope so. She deny nobody happiness when it come to the sex zone.

Maybe she throw out the preacher idea. She throw in a good sex authority, Mama Tuddi will win all the rating wars.

TV come a long way, now that it have a woman at the wheel. Plus her radio show going along clippity-clop.

Come to the menfolks question, there's one over at Sunbonnet, maybe Mr. Sunbonnet himself, who's been itching to have a go at her. You see a man with that itch, that's about all you see. They ain't a whole person the way LeRoy is.

But maybe she give him a nudge.

Maybe she wiggle her finger one little bit.

One wiggle and they's over you like a dump truck.

Lordy, listen to me. I'm gitting a big itch myself, just thinking about them.

The criminal now, she wonder what kind of love life he have. If maybe that why the clutches of the law have got him.

Maybe sometime today they put him on the stand. Maybe then she hear how it happen, whatever it was, without all this mumbly-jive. Maybe then she will take this cotton out of her ears.

It a sad day when a woman of her station have to put up with monkey business like this.

Still, she kind of glad she come. It giving her a bushel of ideas for the new format. She maybe will push to git a new film set, another camera or two, maybe she will run a courtroom-type show.

She get herself a nice bench built, and then she be the judge.

It right peaceful, now she got it all worked out. Cotton wads is tacky, she say that herself, but a woman in these hard times got to do what she must.

Her hair cover it anyway. Nobody in this burg know a thing.

Typical Day in a Desirable Woman's Life

Think *sparrows*, the woman said.

I was mad at this woman. I didn't want to be in the same room with her.

Big deal, she said. I feel the same. Think *sparrows*.

I thought sparrows.

Good, she said. Now describe them.

I described them. I had about five hundred, all locked up in her bedroom. They'd been in the room for days and days, without food or water.

Stop that! the woman said. She was angry, but got control of herself and managed a tight little smile. I admired her ability in this direction. I was learning from her every day.

Come, she said. Come with me.

She got up from her chair and I followed her out of the room.

What do we do about the sparrows? I said.

Close the door, she said. She snapped that out, angry again.

I walked about five paces behind her, down the hall, keeping this distance so I could study how she moved. I wasn't angry anymore. I was quite enchanted with how she moved. I would have been willing to follow her for years and years.

At the front door she turned and waited for me and hooked her arm in mine.

My skirt is too tight, she said.

I love it, I said. I love that skirt.

That is *not* why women in countless societies, age upon age, have walked behind their men. I promise you a tight fit had nothing to do with it.

I know, I said. Give me credit for knowing something.

You don't get any credit, she said. You are absolutely void of all credit.

Why is that? I said. That, it smacks me, is terribly unfair.

Who cares? she said. Someone has got to carry the burden for all that's been done to us, age upon age. Why not you?

Because I'm innocent, I said.

You are *an* innocent, she said, but that's a different matter. Look what you've done to those poor sparrows!

But those sparrows don't exist, I said. Those sparrows are only in my head.

Yes! she said. My point precisely.

She went on down the steps and out across the front lawn.

Don't walk so slowly, she said. Show a little zest. We've lots of time together, all you want, if you will only show a little improvement somewhere along the line.

I am improving, I said. I'm improving every minute.

Tripe, she said. What tripe! I have to spell out every little advance you make. Now quit dawdling.

I sped up, matching her pace. It was true, I'd been dawdling. I loved walking behind her and wished it could go on forever.

No, you don't, she said. You've only wanted to get in my bed. I've known that about you from the first instant.

But only to hold you, I said. We wouldn't have to do anything.

She laughed. She'd heard that one before.

She seated me on a stone bench within a thin quad of trees. We could hear a rippling stream nearby, but couldn't see it.

She lifted an arm onto my shoulder.

Now pay attention, she said.

I sat a bit more erect. She was standing directly in front of me and with the sunlight behind her I could see the shape of her legs through the skirt. I could see how tightly the skirt clung to her hips.

Stop doing that! she said. God, are you a sex maniac in addition to everything else?

Only when I'm with you, I said.

God! she said. Stop it! Focus on something else. She shook my shoulders, then put a hand under my chin and lifted my face. She was bent over, just above me. I hoped she'd kiss me.

But she turned aside and pointed at the sky.

Listen smartly, she said. I am going to do this only once.

Do what? I said.

I was disappointed she hadn't kissed me. I wanted her to kiss me without stopping, age upon age.

Look, she said. Concentrate on the sky.

I looked. I was trying very hard to do exactly as she said.

Think sparrows, she said.

I thought sparrows.

There were five hundred of them and all back in her bedroom. A few were down on their sides, their little stem legs raised. Others were issuing small disheartened squeaks. They were all over the floor and on her bed. They were already stiff and their feathers dingy. Only a few remained in full spirit, fluttering desperately against window and wall.

Hopeless! she said. Hopeless! Why do I bother with you?

She sank to the bench and covered her head with her hands. She trembled.

And you call that *innocence!* she said. When you bring tripe like that into my bedroom?

I wanted to reach out and touch her, caress her face or hair, perhaps stroke her thighs, but knew this would be a mistake. It would be a terrible mistake, given her current mood.

Current has nothing to do with it, she said. I'm talking about the same thing, *age upon age*.

I see that, I said. I see what you mean.

Imbecile, she said. You make me feel so ashamed.

I'm sorry, I said. I'm rather a hopeless case.

After a few minutes she revived. She yanked a tissue from her skirt pocket and wiped her eyes. She looked at me sternly, but then the sternness vanished.

I know you can't help it, she said. You've inherited all this hopeless muck and can't do a thing about it.

I tried out a smile, and the third or fourth time it came out all right.

Fine, she said. Fine. I see I have no choice but to persevere. Come along.

She stood and gave me her hand and pulled me along behind her. She led me through a copse of trees and up over the grass to a field of flowers in wild bloom, and up towards a treeless knoll.

Then up to another hill, the highest around.

The house, from that angle, seemed ringed in by trees, by holly and vine and hedge. The flowers by the front door were in full bloom and the beds amazingly symmetrical. As if some genius painter, a flamboyant water-colorist, had brought his full talent to the creation of this pretty picture.

We could see a stream winding in and out.

Grazing on a hillside was a hefty, spotted cow.

Are you ready to come to your senses? she said. Are you ready now?

I'm already ready, I said. I've been ready since the first minute I caught sight of you.

She drifted a fair distance away from me. I saw her stand on a large outcrop of rock, with the vista empty behind her, the sun shining through her skirt. The skirt was wonderfully tight over her hips, but her legs were naked in the sun and I could see her breasts as well.

We must be completely professional about this, she said.

I said, Yes. Completely.

I want your rapt attention, she said. I mean *rapt*. Don't bat an eye.

I was trembling. She was too, and it seemed to me I was catching it from her.

If this fails, she said, I want never to see you again. I want you out of here, without even the smallest goodbye.

I promise, I said. I'm as good as gone, the minute this fails.

Why should it fail? she said. You are the most negative creature on earth.

I was really trembling. I had not the faintest idea what was expected of me, or what she was expecting of herself.

Look, she said. Look at the sky.

I looked.

Think *bird*, she said.

Bird?

Bird, she repeated. Any kind at all.

I thought back to the sparrows in her room. It was silent and darker inside that room and I couldn't see what the birds were doing.

Bird! she said. Think *bird!* She sounded angry.

I blinked and the sparrow-filled room vanished.

I saw her body lift up and leave the ground.

The sun was dazzling bright behind her, the sky ablaze. For a moment her image blurred and I could scarcely see her at all, only the powerful suggestion of her, as though lit by some impossible radiance streaming in from afar.

She spun and tumbled, she glided and soared.

Are you thinking *bird*? she said.

Bird and you, I said.

I was, too. This was amazing. She was a beautiful woman bird.

She glided right and left. She swooped low and swerved up high again, then hung all but motionless in the air.

I was up on the rock's highest point, reaching for her.

Forget it, she said. You're a clod with concrete in your shoes. Even the smallest flutter is beyond you.

She laughed.

She flew high and low. She was up there, flying all over the place.

Think *sparrow*, she said.

I did. But it was just her usual room. All her windows were open now, a soft wind blowing through, the sparrows gone.

I told her so.

Thank God, she said. If you had killed one single bird, I would never have forgiven you.

She dropped back down to earth. The strange light faded away and the sky behind her was just the normal sky of another pretty day.

Our arms went around each other; we pulled each other close.

I didn't know you could fly, I said.

Only this once, she said. Only under the most critical need.

We stayed on until the sun dropped and lost its rosy hue.

Are we past that little quarrel now? she said. Have I enlightened you even a little bit?

I am totally enlightened, I said. I am a completely new guy.

Christ, I hope so, she said. Now can we go? I am dead-tired.

She went on ahead of me, back through that way we had come.

Then she went through the house, turning on this and that lamp. She was sweaty, she said. She would take a hot, soapy bath.

I sat in a cane chair, in her kitchen, looking at the white walls, listening to a richness of birds at chirp in the near trees: wondering what was going through her mind up there; wondering what else she could do.

Shut Up

"You must do me the favor of doing me the favor of shutting up." That is what she said. It is how she talks. I told her not to talk that way. Talk human, I told her. "When it comes to that," she said, "you don't talk so straight yourself. No you don't." Please stop talking like that, I said. "Talk, talk," she said. "That's all I ever hear. Why don't you be Q.U.I.E.T.? Why don't you Shut. Up?"

That is how she talks: have I made my point? It is how her tongue moves. Not that she is always so rude.

In my adult life years and years have gone by without anyone telling me to shut up. In kindergarten when I was five I was always being told to shut up. This was because I hated kindergarten. I wanted to be at home. At home, my mother never told me to shut up.

That was one sweet woman, that woman, my mother.

Now this one tells me to shut up. Shut. Up. Over and over. Like that, she tells me. You can hear the clock ticking, and the cat meowing, and the floor creaking, between the Shut and the Up.

You can hear civilization's big feet stalking the corridors: that's what you can hear.

Don't talk to me that way, I tell her. Please don't.

"Talk, talk," she says. "That's all I hear is big talk. Have you bought those shoes yet? No? Then Shut. Up."

Now I do not normally watch television. I am a normal person, but I do not normally watch it. As a matter of fact, I hate it. That is how normal I am. In a normal year, say six or seven times I will watch television. That is, at most, in a year, I will live no more than six or seven hours in front of a television set. I do this only to determine whether I still hate it, and not once have I determined otherwise.

The truth is, I much prefer to sit at my desk and stare at a blank sheet of paper. A good ink pen in my hand. It does not have to be my pen – it can be her pen or my son's pen – though I do like it to be my paper and my desk.

"That TV is too loud."

I said that. I definitely said that. Such is how these present difficulties got started. It did not seem to me a mean thing to say.

But both of them thundered into my room, stood before my desk, and in unison, in the meanest of voices, said, "Shut. Up."

That is how our troubles got started. It is the whole story.

Or nearly. For, once they had spoken, a large black figure strode into my room. A large, INERT black figure, once it had got where it was going.

Huge.

We – all three of us – were cast under its spell. Such an ENORMOUS black figure. I had never imagined such a figure could be so large. I could not imagine how, even crouching, it could have come through the front door.

We were under its spell. I said that. We could not say a word. We no longer could see each other. That's how black it was.

I was frightened. I can not speak for my wife and child,

but I definitely was – definitely – in the grip of terror. I thought: I've lost my sight. I can see nothing except this darkness, this blackness.

I was a blind man, that's how black everything was.

But then I thought: Now, what is it exactly that a blind person sees? Do they see blackness, or nothing?

And I felt a little humbled, recognizing that I had gone through my entire life without knowing the simple answer to that simple question.

Gordon, I told myself, when this is over, if it is ever over, you're going to have to ask someone about that.

At that point my wife spoke up. Leave it to her to find her voice first. In the blackness, under the shade of this gigantic fellow, I heard her say, "Is that clear?" And my son saying, "Yeah, Dad, is that clear?"

As if they were totally ignorant of this giant figure blackening the room.

Quite amazing, I thought.

Well, I thought, they lead charmed lives.

Next I heard a shuffling of feet, this and that little sigh of satisfaction, and they left the room. Then IT, that colossal and most *ebon* of creatures, it too slid or strode or somehow left the room, and the room was at once restored to its former familiarity: my desk, the paper, somebody's pen.

What just happened? I said. What's going on around here?

For I wasn't blind anymore. I could see easy as the next guy.

But what I mean when I say I said that is that I must have screamed it, because in an instant they were screaming back, and the TV was screaming, and our dog – as quiet a little pup as ever walked this planet – was barking at full bark, with the result that the entire household seemed to have undergone transformation from normal to bad to worse, and what I said then was as follows:

None of us can go on this way.

This has gone on far too long.

Matters have got out of hand.

It is a madhouse around here.

We have an epidemic here.

Some sanity must be restored.

Can't a person relax one minute?

What is the point of life if this is how it must be lived?

Are my expectations too high?

So I sat there for some minutes, stunned. In a deep haze.

The TV set screaming.

Shoes.

Something about shoes.

I looked out of my window and I saw that where that big black figure had gone was outside. Yes, he was outside now. You can say it was just NIGHT out there, because this did take place at night, but what I say is, I know the difference.

So I got up from my desk and put on my jacket and went outside, intending to have a word with that fellow. Intending to tell him that he was not welcome around here anymore. Intending to tell him that no matter what your size or how impressive your credentials, you couldn't just walk inside a place and take over.

I wanted to tell him, There's a child in there! You take it easy, buster, and consider the consequences of your importunate behavior.

You want to warp childhood?

Intending to say something to him like that.

But the minute I put my head out the door he clapped this big arm over my shoulder and draped a black bag over my head. I went instantly blind again, and I heard him say, "Follow me."

You're kidding, I said. Follow you where?

I stood there, flailing my arms, trying to get that black bag off.

"To the shoe store down on Eighty-third Street," he said. "Stop struggling."

I said: I can't walk. I said: You have a terrible effect on me. I said: How much are these shoes going to cost me?

He said: "Never you mind. I'm going to pay for these shoes myself. Good leather, up to two hundred dollars."

So it happened just the way he said it would: he got me there and he got me back, and now I've got these new shoes and it didn't cost me one red cent.

But the wife accepts none of this. She says, "What big black figure? Have you gone crazy? Can't you admit to the simple act? That you bought those new shoes? No? Then Shut. Up."

Okay, it's how she talks, I've told you that.

Rude.

She claims she has been telling me for months it wasn't civilized how I went about in my old shoes. She claims the television was advertising this gigantic clearance sale on shoes down at the store on Eighty-third Street and that I showed rare good sense and went down and bought a pair. "You could do that by yourself, couldn't you?" she says. "You didn't need any big black man holding your hand, did you?" she says. "Don't answer, just Shut. Up." That's why she and my son had the TV volume turned that loud, she says. So the message could penetrate. "That was my whole and entire aim and object.

"Get with it," she says. "Hang loose. Do me the favor of doing me the favor of never speaking again about any of this business.

"No more of this talk about blind men, or black men! Nothing!"

In other words: "Shut. Up!"

Right.

So now my son wears my old shoes. He likes them, he says. Took them out of the garbage. He says he's going to wear them forever.

"You're not," she says. "Those shoes are disgraceful."

"They are wonderful shoes," he says.

"Already," he says, "I've been offered money for these shoes.

"With these shoes I am the darling of my schoolyard."

She says to him: "People will think you are a beggar!"

He says: "I don't care."

She says: "Shut. Up. Shut. Up up up!"

So the two of us, my son and I, we just sit in his room of nights, him looking at his shoes and me looking at mine. Until that big black fellow strides in and takes it upon himself to sit all around us.

Are you still there, son? I ask.

"What's happened?" he says. "It's gone and got dark."

He's all over the house now, that big ape. Walks in any time he pleases.

You're sitting there and suddenly the room goes black. You stumble down the hall into another room and that one is black too.

The whole house is.

"No, you can't watch any more TV," I hear the wife telling my boy. Then silence. And I know even the TV has gone black, that this black giant is getting bigger every minute, that pretty soon he aims to take over the entire universe.

I sit in my room watching the blackness. Thinking, Is this what a blind person sees?

"Get up here fast!" the wife calls. "Warm these sheets! Christ, must a woman do it all?"

I've told you: that's how she talks.

So I limp up slowly, careful not to knock over anything. I lie there in bed looking at the dark look back.

"Take off your shoes, Gordon," she says.

But I can't find my feet, that's how blind I am. That's how bad matters have got around here.

In the night I wake up sometimes and she's bent over me, she's got an elbow in my ribs; for a minute I see something: her there, with this little pencil light, an eye doctor's little pencil light, beaming this little pencil light into my eyes.

"Don't pretend!" she says. "You saw that! I saw your eyes move! You goddamned miserable squirt!"

And so it goes. Sometimes, some days, the big black figure is gone, some days he isn't. You can't trust him.

One thing I've learned is that he's got his favorite rooms.

"Okay, okay," she says to us. "Enough! You've heard the last word out of me you'll ever hear about shoes. Let your shoes rot. Let your shirts rot, your very hides, let it all rot! Look after yourselves from here on out!"

"Be a bunch of deadbeats!" – that's what she says.

My son and I, we sit in his room.

What do you see? I ask him.

"Nothing," he says. "I'm blind. You?"

In the meantime she goes on about her business. We *think* she does. Hard information is not easy to come by. You ask her a question and she doesn't answer. The silent treatment, that's what we're getting. She has Shut. Up.

Pretty screwy business, all in all.

Drivers

My son asked could he drive my sports car. I said no. No, you can't drive my sports car. He said, That doesn't add up. Why can't I drive your sports car? I said, Because I want to drive it myself. He said, That doesn't add up. You're not going anywhere. I might, I said. I might go somewhere. My wife said, Do the shopping. Go to the bank. Drive over to Elora and buy some Ulisco pears. I said, Jesus! All the way to Elora to buy pears? My son said, He can't go to Elora to buy pears. Leave the man alone. I said, You can't have my car. He said, That doesn't add up. Look, he said, I've just last night got back together with my girlfriend. Today's a new day. So let me celebrate with your sports car. I said, No. No, I said, I've got to do the shopping, got to go to the bank. Now I've got to go all the way to Elora to buy Ulisco pears. My wife said, What's this? You suddenly don't like Ulisco pears? Who have I been living with? My son said, Quieten down, you two. None of this adds up, he said. You never use your car. Probably going to rain anyhow. Who wants pears? he said. We're all sick of pears.

I said, Use your own car. Why can't you use your own car? He said, Hey, come on! It's been three days since I used your car. You can use my car. What's wrong with you using my car? I said, I don't like your car. I like my car. My son

119

said, That doesn't follow. None of this is following. I said, No. Absolutely not, I said. Drive your own car.

He banged around a bit, and went out of the house and got into his car. We heard him gunning the engine and then heard the tires squawling as he spun off. You're right, my wife said. It's foolish to drive all the way to Elora for pears. Shun the pears. Forgive me for ever thinking we liked Ulisco pears. You could do the laundry instead.

We heard a crash. Distant, but near enough.

What's that? my wife asked.

Nothing, I said. Probably the weather-vane falling again. God, the winter we've had around here.

My wife was snitching a look out of the window. I don't think she was feeling any too good about me.

I can't *believe* this, she said. This is the first day he's back with his girlfriend. I *like* that girl. You're a fuckhead for not letting him have your car.

I *never* have my car, I said. My car has been up on blocks all winter. I *never, never* have my car.

Fine, she said. Fine. But if it snows again, don't think I'm going to let a selfish brute have *my* car.

We went out the side door and saw our son walking up the driveway. He looked a bit shaken, but he didn't have a tire hanging around his neck.

Now can I have your car? he said.

I threw him the keys. He got in and drove off.

My wife got in her car and gunned the engine.

Hey, I said, what about me? What about those pears?

LR Loves GL

When I put it in she said Is it in yet? Now that nearly killed me, that was the worst experience of my life, when she said that.

Is it in yet? And I said No, I said No, of course I said No, I said No, it is not in yet, wait a minute.

Hold on, I said.

Well, put it in there, she said.

What could a boy do?

So I put it in harder, it was already in there, but I put it in harder, and she didn't say anything, didn't even blink. Sort of looked around.

So what I did was pretend it had fallen out. If it had fallen out, I had in mind I could pretend to start over, that's what I had in mind by pretending it had fallen out.

Not that I did, for finally she said, after a few minutes she said, after chewing her nail awhile, she said Is that far as it will go?

Yeah, she said that, though she didn't seem the least teensy bit interested, not zap-interested, not even ho-hum interested, and I figured I'd better not pull that It fell out routine or I'd never get it back in again in the first place, that's what I figured.

Far? I said. You want far? You haven't seen far yet, I said, and I gave a big thrust, practically broke my hip bones, that's how big my thrust was. And did it again, maybe three times, maybe as many as five times, hard to tell now, because what I had in mind was Am I breaking my hip bones or not breaking my hip bones? All the time wishing we could sit down a minute, know what I mean? Talk this over.

She grinned, what with all my thrusting, this big grin, and I began to think This is going to work out, Yeah, this is going to work out. Maybe you don't want to sit down after all, that's what I was thinking, but then she said Maybe your finger would do better.

My finger?

My *finger*? Was she out of her mind? I remember thinking that, thinking Is she out of her mind, she can't mean my finger. Sure, a finger is all right, I thought, a finger is fine, nothing wrong with a finger, but did she think I was going to stick my finger up there? Heck, I thought, a finger is your own self, it's like your own self, you use those fingers a thousand times a day, everybody can see your fingers, heck, your fingers are second to your eyes and lips and nose. I wasn't about to stick my finger up there. Would I stick my finger up a place where I couldn't see what was up there? Would you stick it in some knothole in a tree or in a deep hole in the ground? You wouldn't, would you?

Well, I wouldn't. Not in a month of Sundays. Not ever.

In all of this I almost let it fall out, I was that worried.

She had me so worried. Was a guy supposed to be so worried?

So scratch fingers, that's what I'm getting at.

Don't *think*, that was the other thing I was thinking. Don't think, you'll get mixed up, and mess this up. That was an actual thought that went through my head, I promise you it did. And it went through visually, I mean, like an actual thing I could see, those words. *Quit thinking.* In my head, like my little train running along its tracks. My little Lionel with the black locomotive and the red caboose, my little flagman there by the station to wave it on or slow it down. That thought, *Don't think*, just as clear up there in my head as the train was sometimes when I slept.

How it is you can dream these things you like so much.

Whereas below. Below, I wouldn't put my finger in any-thing there, no matter who said it, not even if God on High said it.

God *wouldn't*, that's the point to make on that. And if He did say it, I'd have to say No, God, I'm not putting my finger in any place I know the rest of me can't go, because my finger is my own self and where *it* goes, *I* go.

I'd have to say it to No Matter Who.

Not that He'd say it. I figure he's a guy feels the same way about his fingers as I feel about mine.

She is gnawing on that fingernail. Chewing this thumb.

Can it move? she says. Can you make it move? Maybe you should use a stick.

So help me, that is what she said.

Beg your pardon? I said.

I mean, give me credit. I am not that kind of person.

Sure, you can stick a stick in where you would never think about sticking a finger, but there's a vice-versa side to this stick business, as everyone knows.

Not even if God on High issued the commandment would I use a stick.

All this is going through my mind, like my little Lionel train with the figure-eight track.

Choo-choo. It did this little choo-choo sound, and little puffs of smoke from the engine, like what that engine had riding in it was a bunch of Indians.

I'd forgotten that about the smoke, until this minute. And

those Indians, I always knew there were Indians secretly riding that train.

The little flagman would wave his flag, saying *Stop, washout ahead!* – but those Indians they would toot right on by.

Not a toot, I said that, but a sweet little "Choo-choo."

My point is I wasn't about to consider sticks.

There are some ideas a fella just will not entertain.

What I mean is, for me it was this simple: would you stick a stick up your nose? No, you wouldn't. It was that simple.

Get busy, she says.

I thrust hard as I could. I practically bent myself double. I must have thumped her back a full foot, that's how hard my thrust was. I lost a shoe, that's how hard. Lifted right up out of it, and had to sort of drag it up with a toe and get my foot back inside secretly so she wouldn't notice.

La la, she said.

After all my work, that's what she said.

La la.

After my mighty effort, and dragging up that shoe.

La la.

I tell you, that made me mad. I didn't care whether I fell out or not. I wished I *would* fall out. How much can people expect? That's what I was asking myself.

Suppose you told me those were not real Indians, or real play-Indians, sending up that smoke out of my train engine, out of my Lionel, do you think I'd care? Suppose you told me That's silly. I wouldn't care. I wasn't *expecting* anything of those Indians and if they did or did not send up their smoke puffs and tooted on by the little flagman trying to wave my train down that would not have changed my feelings about those Indians one little bit. I *liked* those Indians. They could do whatever they wanted to. I had put them on that train but if they wanted to get off and go back to their regular life as Indians that was their business and I wouldn't blame them in the least bit. Not the least.

And the same with the little flagman.

My point is, I wasn't making up rules for these people. These were *their* rules.

They liked it exactly the way it was, the way we played it, that's my point.

There was one little tree always falling over, there was that tree.

I had to lean that tree against the station house, but otherwise I got no bellyaches when it comes to me and that Lionel set.

La la. She said that.

And, frankly, to put it bluntly, at that point I fell out.

Those Indians had it easy, compared to what I was going through. Making little puff-smokes, fooling the little flagman, how hard could that have been?

Those Indians could outwit that flagman one hundred times out of one hundred. Every day of the week.

Scratch scratch.

You can just stop your horsing around, that's what I said.

I am not just kidding.

You better watch out.

You're trying my temper, that's what I said.

You've gone too far, I said.

Because what she was doing, and she was really doing it, was writing on that icy, filthy glass

LR

LOVES

GL

Now maybe *you* don't know what that means, but I knew what it meant, and my parents would know what it meant, everybody in my family would know what it meant, and people just walking by on the street, boys I knew, they would know what it meant. And you couldn't miss it either, walking by on that street, because it was right at foot level and the one thing you *would* see, passing our house, which everyone did, maybe a thousand a day, passed our house, because there was a grocery store right across the street on the corner and if you wanted groceries that was the choice, that store, plus our window with these scraggly letters carved in the dirt and frost, LR LOVES GL.

Why didn't she make it GL LOVES LR, that would have been better, that I could have tolerated, but I couldn't tolerate the other any more than I could put up with people saying, my folks saying, those weren't real Indians, real play-Indians in my Lionel engine sending up their puff-smokes and making their "Choo-choos," any more, for that matter, than I could their saying mine wasn't a real train or the little flagman wasn't. They could say that about the tree, they could talk until blue in the face about that tree and none of that bothered me any, but, frankly, well, frankly, I guess what it is that upsets me most is why they have these *compulsions*, these insane impulses to say Those Indians aren't really in there, you know, what's in there, son, if anyone is in there, is just your regular engineer type fella, maybe your coal man, your assistant engineer, but certainly not Indians, no, the Indians are out there in their teepees or on the war trail.

I admit it, I'd get blue in the face, I'd race across the room to wherever they were when they talked like that and I'd ram my head into their stomachs, I'd try my best to knock them over, just shut them up. Because did I need that? Did I need that? Wasn't it my train? Wasn't it given to me? Wasn't it mine to do with as I wanted to and not have to explain anything I did with it to anyone in the whole world if I didn't want to?

Not even to God. If God showed up and said what they
said I'd ram my head into his belly too. And He'd deserve it,
maybe He'd deserve it more than they did, because wasn't
He supposed to know everything?

What I think is He doesn't. I think He doesn't know anything. I think He's so stupid he can't see straight, that's
what I think.

Either that or he doesn't know beans about trains. About
your Lionel set.

You better quit.

You better quit that.

You better quit it right now.

That's what I said, but how long does it take to write four
initials in a frosted-up glass? About two seconds, that's
how long. By the time you've complained it is all over and
what you're left with is the accomplished deed.

How long it takes is about how long it takes people you
know to say what it is they say about those Indians. And
after they've said it, what can you do? You can ram your
head into their stomachs, but it's still said. It's still done.

And the Indians know it. Don't tell me the Indians don't
know it. And the little flagman, you ought to see him. Boy,
he's full of himself, after they've said that. He's all happy
and jumping. He's got that flag waving. If they're not Indians then what's the problem? Your regular type engineer,
isn't he going to obey those flags? Would he risk racing
right through them? No, that flagman is one happy guy.

So the Lionel wasn't any fun then. Just anybody's old
dull train with a hokey figure-eight track.

Like that tree, that's what I mean.

Whereas that tree, by itself that tree was all right. I got
used to seeing it lean. Maybe I liked it.

If she'd only put her own name first. I might have liked
that. I might have felt, you know, honored. Because she'd

let me put it in and hadn't once said anything about its falling out. She was nice. But when she wrote our initials up on that glass what I thought was she was taking the law in her own hands. She was asking for trouble.

Scratch scratch.

It was for the Indians I did it. For them, and to get their revenge on everyone who had said those things. An Indian's wouldn't fall out. If I knew anything at all about Indians, and I knew a lot, I knew theirs never would fall out.

That train could jump that track a thousand times and not once would you see those Indians get upset.

My only thought was I'd butt her, I'd butt her then it would be over, or as nearly over as it was in my hands ever to make it be over. I've told you how I feel about my hands. My fingers are my real self, whereas that thing that falls out, what can it ever pick up? The way fingers can? It can't pick up anything. Any idiot can see how funny it looks. Why she'd say Put it in, Is it in yet is beyond my understanding in the first place. If anybody tried putting one in me I think I'd just croak. I'd keel over. I'd puke, to tell the truth.

Maybe I should have put my finger in. Or that stick.

Because she's been scratching in that frost again and what that window now says is

LR

LOVES

GL

– And Has Proved It!

So I butted her.

What we should have done when she came over was to sit down with my Lionel set. She could have had the other control box. I wouldn't have minded. The other control box couldn't make the puff-puff or do the "Choo-choo," it certainly didn't have the Indians, but she could have come up with something. And we'd never have come up with that It goes in here business. That You put it in here business.

Or there's this:

I knew we had those cookies upstairs. The whole time, I knew it. And on which shelf and how you could take a whole handful and load up your mouth and fold that paper back and no one be the wiser.

There's a cookie thief in this house, that's what my mom was always saying. One of us around here is a cookie thief. But never pointing the direct finger.

And there's this:

I am wet down there. I have gone from wet and cold down there to *frosted*. But can I touch it? With these fingers? To put it back inside my pants? Then go upstairs and eat cookies with the same hand or hands as have touched it? Don't be crazy. God could say Do it and I'd have to tell Him *YOU* touch it! Go ahead, you've got all the ideas, let's see *YOU* do it. And if I know God, I know he wouldn't. He'd say You get that thing back inside however you can but I don't want anything to do with it.

Leave me out of this, he'd say.

Because there's not that much difference between God and me, between God and the next person, is how I feel about it.

I butted her, but I insist I didn't hurt her.

Not that much. Not how much she says.

Then there's the big fuss, with parents running and everyone squawking, and mostly I just hung my head and kept trying to sneak off. But they kept stopping me and shaking me and saying things like Did you? Did you hurt this child?

What kind of monster are you?

And I'm thinking, They know. She's told them. Our lives are ruint now.

But she hadn't told them.

What got me was when they finally eased up, and said Honey, you go over and hug her. You two show each other you've got no hard feelings.

Forgive each other, that's what they are saying.

And you got to. You got to or you can't go to bed, you can't have a cookie, you can't have your Lionel, you can't ever have anything.

Now kiss each other, they say.

On the mouth.

There are no limits, that's my point. Aren't lips like your hands? Don't lips have a purpose in life plain as the purpose of hands?

Whereas, down there. Is that what they want next? To see me put it in? To see will I fall out?

Sticks?

Is *that* what they want?

Extracts from the Proceedings of the Annual Meeting of the Huron Street Benevolent Society

Unreliable Narrators

This old man on crutches showed up, looking his years, and said he was going to tell us the world's greatest story. We said, Tell it, Fred. So Fred started in telling his tale, and after the longest while we said, What's happening, Fred? This here story sounds like you're still where you were in the beginning. When do we get to the good part?

That's right, said Fred. But I am only telling it to you how it was told to me, since that's how the world's greatest story gets told.

Who'd you hear this story from? we asked Fred. Was it some other old guy? Did he die of fatigue, or was it boredom did him in?

Yeah, said Fred. Maybe he died.

I was a young man then, said Fred, and can't perzackly remember.

All I know, said Fred, is that this old guy told it to me said he'd got it from some other old guy, and it had been going on for ages.

For ages? we said. The world's greatest story?

Yeah, said Fred.

Then he waved his crutches about, not liking these interruptions one bit, and went on telling the story.

One by one we started drifting out, because it was turning out this story was long and boring, and short on the surprise angle, and – you could say – utterly familiar.

Fred said, Yeah, as a youngster just coming into the picture, that had been his precise reaction. Plus it won't even the whole truth. It won't even the *half*-truth, come to that, Fred said. Frankly, it had a lot missing.

But he went on telling the story.

Then this woman over by the window, been fuming at us the longest time, stops fiddling with the drapes. You can see she's stewing. What she says is, Drop dead, Fred.

Say your goodbyes, guys.

So she jumps in with *her* story.

And at just that point, the tale suddenly became interesting. We were suddenly, all of us, *tuning in*.

The Bucket Brigade

My husband awakened me from a deep sleep.

"No one can tell," he was saying, "how much I have suffered. Day in and day out, endlessly and silently, over the years."

"Not silently," I said. "Go and get your bucket."

And I went back to sleep.

But a little later I was again awakened, by his tossing and turning, by the droning monotony of complaints. By his chronic whines. By his boasts. By *my* life, as *he* saw it.

"You are the apple of my eye," he was saying. "My solace, my comfort, my cheer. But I wonder how I can go on in the face of these abiding aches. These pains! Why me? Why must I be the one to suffer, without relief? I have two brothers, you know, who have never suffered one stinking minute. And my sisters did all right, too, excusing, for purposes of this conversation, the sorry wretches they married. Now that is just within my immediate family. If I consider others I have known, friends, I mean to say, I have to conclude that their plight, their suffering, does not begin to compare with mine. Look at my job! Imbeciles get all the pay, but consider who does the work! Consider that."

I flung myself from the bed, flicked on the light, and went and got his bucket.

"Now," I said. "Now may I go to sleep? "

I squirmed into bed and smacked off the light.

But he immediately hoisted himself high upon the pillows. He continued to insist on talking to me.

"So much has gone wrong with my life," he said, "for which I am not to blame. No, I think I am blameless on all fronts, but still I am made to suffer. If there is trouble afoot anywhere, you can be sure it will come my way. Look at the behavior of my parents, for instance. Their actions toward me have been most peculiar, to say the least."

I leapt in dismay from the bed and placed the bucket securely in his hands. I swung the wire handle over his head and shoved his face in.

"Use your bucket," I said. "That is why I *got* you this bucket, and you will use it *now!* "

And with that remark I jumped back into bed and fell into precious sleep.

Periodically during the night I could hear him recounting his misfortunes, the ragged litany of his perceived ill-luck – could hear him reciting the whole of his imagined sorrows – into the bucket. But these came to me as far-away whispers might, as soft music almost, and in no way disturbed my dreams.

In the morning, I said, "Empty your bucket," and he looked at me with glazed eyes, but went away and did so.

The same now, each evening. "Not a word," I say, "without your bucket."

"It is not precisely a bucket," I have told my friends. "No, it is, more precisely, a nice yellow pail. And I am happy. All is bliss, all is perfect tranquillity, since I got him his bucket."

Which is why, yesterday, you may have seen so many women on our street scurrying about the neighborhood. Poking their heads into hardware and department stores, into Jane's Place, and Honest Ed's. "Have you a bucket?" they cried. "A nice yellow pail?"

And scorching their paths home, dashing into their bedrooms, setting up their buckets, excited and uplifted by the sudden promise life offered them.

Lunch Detail

When Claire married the lunatic she did so with a clear head.

"I knew what I was getting into," she said to her pal Joyce, both splashing back wine – "What a lazy day!" – during a thoroughly unappetizing lunch at the Bright Street Café.

Joyce giggled. She'd been a giggler since the day she first could walk, and she'd forever be one.

Claire hated it when Joyce giggled.

"What a lunatic he is," she said. "This morning, do you know what he did? He threw the cat three hundred yards, one end of the house to the other. Yes, poor kitty. The cat shot right across my nose, a black spear. No, don't giggle, Joyce. All because there was no bread for his precious toast. No eggs, either. No fruit, no cereal. The kitchen, now that I mention it, is practically empty, save for a few canned goods no one liked. Do you ever use that expression 'Save for'?"

Joyce giggled. Oh, she was at full tilt today.

"We're having a bet on, you see. Whoever goes to the supermarket first, loses. I think he's breaking. He's on the ropes. He knows he's going to lose and it's making him more neurotic and lunatic and beastly than ever."

"What does the winner win?"

"What?"

"Your bet. What do you win?"

"Oh, hell, I don't know. Who cares? That isn't the point, Joyce. Of course I'm going to win. It was stupid of him ever to make such a bet in the first place. He's a fool, Joyce. He doesn't know me at all."

Joyce said, "Excuse me." She'd seen someone she knew, over at another table. She wanted to go over and say hello.

Claire watched her go. What a fatso, she thought. God, am I in a lousy mood today.

She watched Joyce greet the man . . . a volley of giggles. The man embracing her. Another lunatic, you could see that just by how he hugged a person. The idiotic smiles.

Claire jumped to her feet, flinging her napkin down. Her chair tipped back and clattered to the floor. "Why don't the two of you get married?" she shouted. "Tie the knot!" Everyone turned to stare at her. "Yes," she cried, "I can see you two would make a great pair!" She strode through the tables towards the door, noting with satisfaction the astonished faces lifted to her.

"You pay!" she shouted back at Joyce. "Or, better yet, have that son of a bitch fork it over!"

Outside, she discovered a pebble had worked its way inside her shoe. She lengthened her stride. She wasn't about to stop, lean hand against a wall, slide off her shoe and empty it of whatever pebble or rock or giant boulder had got in there. Not with that crazy bunch back there watching her every move.

Poor kitty, she thought. Now they know how you felt.

Even the cafe's name was a lunacy. It wasn't on Bright Street. Fucking Bright Street didn't exist, not in this one-horse town.

Christ, the examples she could think of! – it was like a disease, this absurdity. It was like her goddamn Willie went through the city every day, smearing his brush over everyone.

She stopped at a corner store and bought herself candy bars.

"I've got to eat," she said. "To keep up my strength, if I'm going to be able to handle him."

She'd enter the house with chocolate smeared all over her face, over her hands and in her hair. She'd drop candy wrappers all over the floor.

Would he be home?

God, she hoped so.

She thought: My state of mind is a state of grace.

She couldn't wait – had such a fierce need – to fly home, throw him down, crawl up over him, pin him to the floor. Get her knee up against his crotch.

Do you give up? Will you say you're sorry, now?

But first I'll play with him, she thought. Give him a nice kitty purr.

Mate's Rap

"You win some, then you win some more, then you lose once, once only, and you're ready for the straitjacket." That is what I told my husband after he'd lost, or thought he'd lost, me. To another party. It was what I said to him while I was putting the straitjacket on him.

"Stand still," I told him. "You've been asking for this for a long time, so don't complain now."

"That's right," I said, "hold out your arms. You haven't lost me, I don't know how you come up with these strange ideas. Where this jealously comes from. How you could possibly work yourself up into these manic states."

That is what I told him.

"Wait a second," I said. "Let me tie off these little ends. That's right, darling. Fold your arms over. Fold them comfortably. It's a nice color, isn't it, the whitest white, now don't you get it dirty."

"Turn around," I said, "let me see you. Oh, it's wonderful, I do believe you could win a prize."

"It's snug enough, I hope. Does it feel snug? Step over to the mirror, what do you think? Not too bad, is it?"

"Yes, yes," I said. "Well, it's supposed to feel that way. It would defeat the whole purpose of the jacket if I loosened it, now wouldn't it?"

"You do have the oddest ideas."

That is what I told him.

"If you lose, or feel you've lost – if you will insist upon it – then you might as well lose hard. How otherwise will you know that what has happened to you has any real meaning in the world?"

"Wouldn't you agree?"

"What other party?" I asked him.

"Where do you get these senseless notions?"

"No, I do not want to hear one word of this evidence you claim to have."

That is what I said to him.

I said, "You can just stay in that jacket until you can think like a reasonable human being."

I said, "Maybe you could plead temporary insanity. I don't know how otherwise you could explain these crazy accusations, these dark suspicions that spin about in your mind like whirlwinds. Creatures, only, of your ludicrous imagination."

"Good," I said. "I'm so delighted that you now have calmed down."

"Exactly," I said. "The world is not coming to an end."

"Yes, yes, we can get you a pair of white shoes to match, if we must. If you insist."

My husband then asked if he could sit down.

I said, "No, no, the very nerve! Sit down at a time like this? When in this household there is drama afoot of unpardonable, indefensible proportion? When you have brought malign turbulence into our love-nest?"

Then he spoke.

My husband said, "All right, Agatha, I can now see there was no justifiable cause for my suspicions, and that I have only made matters worse by going off half-cocked. Forgive me, darling."

I said nothing.

He said, "I can see now that all this was in my nasty mind and that your flirtations were perfectly harmless."

I said nothing.

"And of no consequence," he said.

I said nada.

Then he said nada.

This compromise continued even as I sat down to eat my dinner.

"I'm sorry, darling," he'd say.

And if he were being contrite enough, I would spoon teensy morsels into his mouth.

For the next little while we each went about our own business. I, for instance, made my usual phone call, in which I arranged my affairs pleasingly, for the morrow.

Towards bedtime, he asked whether he couldn't wet his throat.

I said, "Wet your throat, what does that mean?" – for it had an obscene ring to me.

"No, no," he said. "I meant only whether you might be so kind as to let me have a glass of water."

We got into bed.

My arrangements were made for the next day, I could breathe easily. That is something I have learned in my time: *Always, always, assure that you have something pleasant to look forward to.*

And the day, in fact, dawned blue and sunny.

He was still sleeping, his straitjacket white and snug, not at all wrinkled. Looking quite handsome, I thought.

We had breakfast, no surprises there. No complaints. An itch between his shoulder blades, he said, which I soon made right.

No accusations, no charges of disloyalty, cruelty, deviousness; no moaning, hand-wringing, no "where were you on such-and-such night?" – none of that. I felt rather proud of him.

"There you go," I said to him at the door. "Have a nice day at work."

But he loitered, he doddered, he malingered.

"What is it?" I asked him. "What's troubling you now?"

"I hope," I said, "I do so fervently hope that I will hear no more of your 'pitiful me' number. No more of that 'Am-I-losing-you' business."

But I had misjudged the poor man. No, he was only wondering, he was only worried, that people in his office might comment, might inquire, might *speculate* – "Might ask why I am wearing this straitjacket."

"Well, darling," I said, "if you are so concerned, then you might forget about the marketplace and think about staying home to do woman's work."

But he seemed so threatened, so frightened, by this possibility, that I relented and became kindness itself.

So I draped his regular suit coat over his shoulders and rigged his attaché case to his belt. I wheeled him about and gave him a polite shove down the path.

"Kiss-kiss," he said.

I threw mine back at him.

Then I came in and had myself a sumptuous bath. While in the bubbly, I reconsidered my plans. A drive in the country with my friend would be ever so much fun, I thought. Blue skies, a perfect day. Who knew what wonders we might invent for ourselves!

Choirmaster's Report on Dissension in the Holy Father's Ranks

Some women in my choir have lately taken to gross abandonment. They hang about in taverns and on village greens, they lean against lampposts and shout rude remarks to sailors. The Bishop has been protesting and I have here his latest official directive: "It has come to my attention yet again . . . " Yes, that kind of letter. "Dire consequences, etc., etc." I am perfidious, lax, permissive, my faith has slipped: that is what the Bishop hints. But he has his own troubles. He knows now that he will never become a cardinal, a pope, never claim an important chair in heaven or jog on earth among the front-running saints. "A bishop's a little piece," he tells me on the phone. "You think you're insignificant, yet you don't know what the word means, no one ever does, unless they reach certain heights. It's only at certain elevations that you come to know how soundless are our footsteps on the ground. Up here where I am, I tell you, the air is thin as well."

So he knows perfidiousness from the inside, the slack hours when faith is undernourished and strong drink, the reproof of underlings, is all that ticks his clock around.

The women in my choir hoot and jeer at such disclosures. They vilify him and me and all others occupying the male bastion. "Put a woman in charge," they say. "Isn't it time the little assaulted boys were given a rest?" Oh, they play dirty pool, these women in my choir. Nor will the Bishop let the matter rest. He calls up, his speech slurred, wanting news: "What are your strumpets up to now?" he asks. "What's the latest?"

He alludes piously to the devine infallibility of the gentleman in Rome; he suggests that infallibility accrues as one advances in the ranks. Hierarchy, he says, what else is it for except to separate the sheep from the tyrant, the shepherd from the goats? "Take note, Stubbs," he says. "This is infallible opinion you're getting now, straight from the horse's mouth: at your position, nothing! Zip. You possess all the infallibility of a house-rat devouring cheese. Chomping away at some poor infant's crooked toes. But me? I get the taste. Twenty per cent, I'd say. That's about how much infallibility sticks to me. Though it varies with the bishop, of course. There's give and take. Go on up the ladder and you'll find a cardinal has about fifty per cent infallibility. Otherwise, he's dead wrong. But the Pope! The Pope!" he cries, his voice lifting with zealous pride in which you can detect his own strong dose of ire.

Talking to him, you get the idea, readily enough, of the hideous discord his soul knows as he treads the hallowed soil. At ground level his faith slips and slides, but at the top, where his head resides, is belief as trenchantly secured as our Pope's famous hoarded gold. "Tell that to your choir," he says. "Let the bitches grind their teeth. Let them rant and rave."

"Hey," he says to me. "You ought to come around one of these nights. Let's flap our lips, give report on the vanished, noble days. Who knows, some of my infallibility may rub off. Do it. It's no fun drinking alone."

The women in my choir hoot, they jeer. They have taken up the javelin, the ballista, the arbalest – casque, breastplate, and sword. They practise each night on the village green, each out to make the perfect score. "A bull's-eye every time," that's their goal. They mean to storm the church, to take it by force. They rumble along in armored buckboard wagons to this and that meeting place through the night. Off-duty, they lean against lampposts, their thighs exposed, reeking of scent, their hair-dos flamboyant as wriggly bags of snakes.

Giving the finger to your ordinary citizenry who, naturally enough, dislike the fuss. Taunting sailors. "Hi-ya, pretty boy! Want to have some fun?" Influencing these guileless infidels to abandon ship and take up the sisterly cause. "Yes," they say. "There the solace for you, my sailor-boy; not between my legs."

In the meantime, they sing, these women do. How they sing! They sing as never before. Such hellions they are, their crescendos off the charts. They lift the very spires, the roof, they set the tower bells ashiver, the village green ablaze. Our beautiful cathedral windows are developing cracks, monstrous glivets in the swirly panes; in cold weather I can feel the wind whipping about my neck.

"We've got the faith, baby," say the women in my choir. "You and your bishop, you're faces on the totem; you're the hoary frost of yesteryear. Let justice reign. There you have it, honey: cook and scullion maid's rendered bill for that old cookout, The Last Supper. *Gloria Gloria! Queen of Queens!*"

Sorrows Drowned

When Larry left town, or was sent packing, Avis, the woman who sent him, was pairing herself with a shortened, hunked fellow named Slyde. Named that, Larry said, after a lizard, this Slyde character affecting a limp when people were watching, but who could move pianos, Larry said, if you saw him true. Slyde, in a matter of days, in fact overnight, had become a regular home-husband to Avis, an ear-nibbler any time they sat on the couch, with guests assembled, drinking out of the bottle there on the low table.

Out of the bottle, Larry noted, he'd provided.

Slyde's boots up on the table too, and Avis all over him. Both of them that way, sticky with each other as a second coat of paint you'd dab on before the first is dry. Consorts, they said, giving meaning to the phrase "home front." Already in warm-ups for wedding bells, so they said, much to the distress of Larry.

"I tell you," Slyde said, his shoes up on the table, "they'd have to invent new skin mags, for what me and this woman do with each other."

Avis beaming.

Larry, his heart broken, shoved to the sidelines, there sharing that bottle with them, since didn't he have the right?

Wasn't he still paying the rent? Aching from the sight of Avis's black-stocking legs slung across the lap of her lizard paramour, Avis nuzzling the fellow. Avis testifying to all and sundry that she wanted, couldn't wait to have, with Slyde, a peepot of – for instance – children. More than her mother, grandmother, all her ancestors rolled into one had ever thought about conceiving. While parenthood with Larry she'd called a peril to be avoided like dreaded plague.

And what Larry – who had a friend down at the Planned Parenthood office, and who had wanted only what Avis wanted – had put up with to prevent conception during that period he and Avis had been one and the same had him now thinking terrorist acts.

"Now him and her, Slyde and Avis," he was given to saying, "are like permanent press. Like something you never even have to take off. Wear it to bed, even. You seen that car they drive? I give her that car. A sporty model. That can hardly hold the two of them, seated or prone unless on top of each other, which is the case, believe you me."

"Get lost, vaminos, pack your bags, split, I'm out of your life," Avis daily, hourly, said to him.

"It's over," she said.

"Quit hounding me."

"Show a little dignity, pal," Slyde said.

He heard such comments from this pair, morning to sunset. Like mortar shots, messages from battlefield HQ, him answering back, lobbing up reminders of all he and Avis had said to each other back in their romantic patch. Promises made, the down payment on the condo, how the very apartment she and this guy Slyde were making out in was still in his name. And who's responsible, anything goes wrong with the garburator, the toilet bowl? Like with the telephone, the utilities, who gets the bills? Note: my dishes, my mop and broom, my CD player.

"My stuff still in there, that this fellow's putting his feet on."

"Sure," Avis would say. "Because you won't come take away your precious goods. Because you can't keep your foot out of the door. Because you're an aggravating, fat-headed pig."

"Larry," Avis would say. "Load this up inside your head. I don't go for you. I never did."

"So bug off," Avis says.

Larry pulls out his checklist: "Aren't the very clothes you are wearing part and parcel of our trousseau? Those black stockings on your legs, didn't I fork over sixteen bucks for those stockings at Holt Renfrew's?"

While the guy, Slyde, his arms around Avis, flops his head from one to the other of them, smiling. Saying, to Larry's mind like unto a bogus hippie creep – "I can't dig you, man. You make my head spin. I see you pleading your case to my love-breath here, and I'm put in mind of that choppy-jawed Godzilla, in the Japanese flick. Returned to life after a million-year freeze in the ice field. Getting all savage, you know? Uprooting whole cities."

And holding out his hand, for what? The keys? Larry is supposed to turn over the keys? To what holds his whole life?

"Fat chance," he says. "I'm holding on to these. Because one of these days Avis is going to see you for what you are."

They show him the wedding licence, the ring.

"We're serious, Larry," they say. "Take a hike, bud."

So Larry finally hikes.

Who Larry has been recounting this tale to, for weeks now, is his new love. He's gone south, and got lucky. "I jumped off the burning deck," he tells her, "and there you were."

But his news, to Rikkie's ears – Rikkie, his new-found lady love – is getting old. She's fed up with this torch Larry won't let burn out.

What she says to him is, "It's not me you love, it's just the idea of love. Of what I represent. No, you're still hooked on her, that's for sure."

"Wrong," says Larry. "I'm out of it, but I want reparation. I want my old apartment back, and all was in it when I left."

"You just want to see her," Rikkie says. "You want her to melt in your arms."

"Wrong," says Larry. "You are my love goddess now."

Which words make Rikkie scrunch up her face. Can't a girl just have a normal relationship with a guy? Can't she be just herself?

As for that, both Larry and Rikkie know she's been running from hard times. From a guy worse, if such is possible, than Slyde. Minus the details, but down in Georgia, where she and Larry met, her in maelstrom heat with this guy given to wearing slim leather neckties and insisting on a low fibre diet. A D.W.I. lawyer who nightly drove out, loaded down with neckbraces, himself sloshed, on his Harley, to wave his lawsuit threats, his Polaroid photos revealing guilt, and to rescue diehard innocent victims from jangled fenders and broken glass. All for his thirty-three per cent of whatever settlement he could get.

"He had no panache, Larry, like I know you have, his goals in life not lofty, as I know yours are, from the saintly burn in your eyes. The way you came on to me all electric heat and sizzly by-products of same. That goofball lawyer was mean to me like I know you can't even think of being."

Her hopping up all birthday-suited, after a three-day downspin, to blink at him, in this seedy motel room where they've lucked across each other. Customizing herself, in the instant, to the new arrangement. Getting friendly with the feeling of unexpected salvation. Hiding from him, who already had dressed them the night before, the slashed wrists on both her arms.`Later in the day, with food under their belts, each probing the other's eyes. Like these four eyes are fitted with some kind of powerful periscope that can answer the questions each other has: Are you real? Can I count on you for at least a little while? Or has someone slipped bad dope under these headbands?

"It's like, before I met you," Rikkie says, "I saw spotlights over the city and the bombers already droning overhead, like in Iraq that time. Must I live with a feeling like that the rest of my life? Or can I count on you and you on me, like dust under the bed? Are you going to moan over that piece forever, Larry? Do I lay here beside you, into eternity, listening to you whisper her name in your sleep?"

"Wrong," says Larry. "My heart is with you, tied with silken threads, but the mind drifts, Rikkie, like – ?"

"Oh, I know, honey-love. The wind, the wind."

Now here's the transpiring.

"Wait up, Larry," yells Rikkie, and here she comes with their suitcases, his panama hat, her hairdryer and curling iron that she's forgot to pack until the last minute. The cord dragging on the sidewalk, and the red tool box she's insisted on bringing. Saying, "Larry, in case you need to learn a trade, though I mean to work too, as seventy-six per cent of my sisters do. Out there vying for bread, seeking sovereignty in the workplace, relief from harassment, wherever relief is."

They are back on what Larry calls his home turf. They are back where, in Rikkie's eyes, Larry can not be his better self. No, he's become some other guy.

"They've got my Sony, Rikkie," Larry says. "My old school report cards. Everything."

So she's feeling down and out, Rikkie is. She's feeling she's going to lose this guy.

"But look," she says, and inside her drawstring purse there's a bottle of fermented grape, of the bubbly sort. To toast the occasion, which is their coming together, finding each other, in what she calls the late rounds. "And not a dribble left over for me, my love, if you see this woman's face and fall in a loveheap into her long arms."

"Wrong," says Larry. "Let's save the uncorking for our first housekeeping, tomorrow, for sure."

Thus, to sweep ahead now, with clock and story conspiring.

We are high in the sky, in the revolving bar at the Tower of Towers, prearranged site for the meeting of these four.

Slyde arrives, groomed to the nines, announcing his ladylove's delayed, she's had to call in a vet to look at her puppy.

"You've got *dogs* now?" asks Larry, and somehow the way he says this causes Rikkie to cry out in distress, and in tears race away to the women's.

Slyde has his feet propped, as is his custom, on the table.

"One," he says, as though more would be offensive. "A puppy."

They drink and say nothing, and have a second one, and still Rikkie stays hidden and Avis does not come through the door.

"Happy?" asks Larry, and what Slyde says in response heightens the mystery.

"Oh, delirious."

Feeling each other out. Neither quite yet willing to jump in with actual feet.

"We've repainted," says Slyde. "You wouldn't recognize the place."

"Oh, yeah," says Larry. "Good for you." But what he's thinking is, Who's still sitting on the lease? Me. Me, me, me.

Avis still doesn't come. Avis is a no-show. The big bar, overlooking the city, continues its slow spin.

Nor, for half an hour now, has Rikkie shown her face. For all Larry knows, she's back there in the Women's, taking razor to her wrists.

So "Excuse me," he says. "I better go check."

Which is how both of them find themselves, a minute later, standing side by side, in the Men's.

What Larry is thinking is, This guy is a hotdog, with sawdust all over his shoulders, yet he eased me out like I was on skateboards. Who is to know the heart's mind?

They are straight-up at the urinals, intent on their business, when Slyde nudges him, and drops his head. And it occurs to Larry that he's being asked to look at something down on the floor where they stand: gum on the tiles, Larry figures, or somebody's spit, maybe some message like you might find spray-gunned on a synagogue. But when he looks there's nothing there. Slyde nudges him again and says, what Larry thinks he says is, "That puppy is maybe bad sick. I think I better maybe scoot on back home, see if them two are needing me."

What Larry does is sink a hand into his pocket and bring out the ring of keys he's been carrying lo these months.

"By your leave, old man," he says. Which remark fills him with instant joy.

Slyde smiles, refusing the keys.

"No matter, sport," he says. "We stowed away your goods and had the locks changed the minute you left town. Me and Avis were tired of you hassling us. No hard feelings, though," he says.

And, just before he goes through the door, Slyde says: "Just so you know: Avis and me are with child. We are gung-ho on this family thing."

And what Larry sees, hearing this, is this pair in a different light. The jealousy, and the little hurt that washes in, is of a different sort.

"Man to man," he says, shaking hands, "I and Rikkie wish you and yours all the luck."

Now Rikkie and Larry, arm in arm, have hit the street.

They are setting off into the future, and feeling good. A feeling of connection, of purpose, in every step.

"What happened," says Rikkie, "is that I and this other woman in the toilet, in our gloom, decided to throw ourselves a party. I uncorked the fizzy. She sat in her stall, I in mine, recounting our stories, passing the bottle back and forth. 'Here's to better days,' she said. That's how she toasted every slurp. Like we were launching our every old heartache into the murky depths."

"Sounds good," Larry says.

"You'd of liked her," Rikkie replies, "though I guess it was mainly a woman's thing."

Right, thought Larry. Me, too. With any luck.

Neighborhood
Watch

I say you can tell a lot about a person by her pets. Delilah, awful name though okay for a pet, didn't have any and I say right there you know enough about her. What woman in her right mind wouldn't like cats? I'd been watching her come and go for about six months, her head in the air like she was riding a train, no time for anybody. Two or three times I saw her in the Supervalu, passing right on by the pet aisle and not spending too long in the housecleaning section either. She didn't eat meats, didn't eat cereals, seemed to have a yen for that tofu stuff and much else I wouldn't try on a bet. One day I was walking behind her, both of us returning home, when this little dog came up and sniffed at her heels and I heard her tell it to shut its yap and scoot. "Back off, dog," is what she said. It didn't and she kicked it: that's the kind of woman she is, doesn't like dogs, does not like cats, thinks she owns the street. This car braked in with a man behind the wheel, she got in and threw her arms around his neck, climbed all over him, then spun on the seat and said, "Look at him, he's the old shit always following me." The man laughed, they spun off, her wedged up under his arm like lice to a feather, the both all giggly, with no mind to the burning issues of the day, only their own pleasure. Later on I see them come up and park in the spot behind her house, way past dark this was, and they get out leaning on each other and go inside and not one light ever does come on.

She wouldn't join Neighborhood Watch either, just said, "Screw that, daddy, there's too much watching going on already."

I figured her about thirty-five, never been married, never would be, probably a regular at the Abortion Clinic, and she damn well hadn't come from any place around here. The wife says to me, Well, do you think she's good-looking, and what I say is, What I think is she ought to have her head examined, she ought to be locked up, anybody would kick a dog. Yes, the wife says, but do you think she's pretty? I give her a long look that ought to tell her to keep her mouth shut because in the first place looks vanish, the wife herself being case one, and in the second place there are more important matters, like adequate funding for the SPCA and all those animal experiments going on in a thousand laboratories where they will cut open a monkey or cat or whatever for no good reason and then throw it in the garburator to be ground up and flushed away. "But do you find her attractive?" the wife insists, this being one of those rare days when she's speaking. Sure, she's all right, I finally tell the wife, though to speak for myself I can't stand women of her physical type, think they're so special when the truth is about a million women got it all over her and even one or two have a warm spot in their hearts for the animal world. But the wife won't let go of it, she gets hold of a topic she thinks she's Krazy Glue, so next she's asking, "Well, name one woman around here you think is prettier." I know what she wants, of course, for me to say she is, but I say that kind of talk went out of this household a long time ago. So I mention another woman across the street, and that takes the wife back because this is someone she hasn't even noticed, didn't even realize a new couple had moved in over there when the Hungarians finally shipped out. "You're impossible," she says, and that, thank God, is the end of that.

Right about here in the time sequence I'm talking about my best cat "Miss Mew" has three kitties, then two more a few minutes later, and another one in the little basket the next morning when I get up and go in for my cereal. The wife says, "With what we spend on cat food around here I could have sent three children to college," and what I say is I could, not you, because I'm the breadwinner in this house. We don't say any more for another hour, the next time I'm aware of her existence is when I see her carrying the kitty basket out to the back doorstep, the mama cat "Miss Mew" yowling, the wife with her feet pointed, this imbecilic laying-down-the-law expression on her face, saying, I'll not have any more cats around here, you get rid of these and that's that.

We have a big fight then, lots of slamming doors, and I can see this is one of those I'm-taking-a-stand-on-this times.

Before I got married I lived alone in this place in the woods, with about two dozen cats, and I had this board I put up against an open window so those cats could come and go as they please, none of that silly little teensy cat-door business, which is demeaning to cats and one of the world's worst ideas.

And take down that awful board, the wife says, I simply am not going to live like that any more. The wind just roars through, she says, and who has to clean up their mess, I ask you.

This is news to me but I can see there's no arguing with her, no use pointing out that she's got the whole half side of the house to herself anyway, that half sealed off from me and the cats, thank God, because we wouldn't want to have any part in it.

But that is not the story. The story is that woman down the street. I marched right up to her door that day, three weeks later it was, the wife gone on an extended stay with her sister, my idea being this woman could take her pick of the two, whichever one most appealed to her, the both of them fluffy and cute and in good health, on their way to being housebroken and cats would improve and enrich any person's life. You can't love a little kitty, I say, who can you love?

So I knocked and waited a good ten minutes. She came to the door wearing this silly garment which I have seen in the ads, a what-you-call-it teddy, which is what you put on apparently to attract or entice a man. She's wearing a pink one, this romp of lace across where her breasts are and another run of it hemming each leg, real tight down there where her crotch is. But I don't take time to notice this, I'm here on business, so I immediately thrust the kitty box in her arms, I say, Here's your precious kitty, just take one if you don't want both.

"Jesus Christ!" she says.

She slings the box one way, the two kitties another, then shoves me all the way out to the street. "Keep your goddamn zoo out of my hair!" she says, screaming that out like she's suddenly gone demented. "The whole goddamn neighborhood is so run over with cats I can't walk straight," she says. "I haven't seen a goddamn bird here in ten years, not since you moved in!" She shoved me again and stalked back inside wild as a gypsy, the little teddy at ride up to her waist, with her legs looking about as tall as stilts and her buttocks jaunty as a pair of sunbonnets.

"Don't bother me again!" she shouts, and slams the door.

Do you think I'm taking that kind of behavior?

I went home and called the law, making no bones about how I felt. "Book her," I said, "I want that little lady booked, I want that bitch thrown in jail, she's dangerous, a public menace!"

"Hold on, sir," they say, "let me take that down."

So I go through the whole story again, three times I give it, and still the moron is saying, "How's that again, sir, let me see if I have it straight."

I can see all they mean to do is pussy-foot around.

"Some folks don't like cats," the guy said. "Did she harm you in any way? Physically assault you? How intentional was this push? You were giving her kitty cats, you say? Have you seen a doctor and have you had good professional photographs taken, color shots would show your wounds? You got any broken bones, a cast on your arms, that would help, that's essential if we are to take this into a court of law. More important, will you stick with these charges and not back away like so many members of the public do? Of course, you could go another route on this deal, and bring a personal suit against her, go for big damages, though I can't advise you on that."

An idiot, not worth giving him my time of day.

I call the wife, I say to her, Can you imagine what has happened to me? Do you know what's going on around here? And she says, "Oh the pretty one was it? Well, I hope she broke your fucking arm!" Then the sister comes on, she's shouting like a lunatic, asking *"What have you done to my sister?"* and other such rubbish, such as how before I came along Little Sis would die rather than use a word like that, and finally the wife is on the line again telling me she's never coming back, not for all the gold on earth. But what gets me most is she's asking me have I named all the new little kitties Delilah, am I letting them sleep in my bed?

156

Jesus Christ!

"Good!" I tell her, "don't come back, have yourself a sweet old time," not that I have an uncaring bone in my body but the truth is I'm in something of a rage. I get my plank back up at the open window for the cats and I empty a full box of dry food into the bowl and watch about a dozen of them go at it, trying to wedge their noses into the bowl and climbing all over each other, hissing and spatting, their claws out, their fur on end, like they're starving creatures hadn't been fed in three weeks, which is one of the wife's complaints, that they are so many they've all gone wild and ought to be rounded up and shot, one by one, a huge *mass grave*, she says, big enough to hold a hundred cats and all your tears. Little irony in the tone, you know, like she's saying I couldn't weep for human beings. That being the burning issue, to hear her tell it.

The phone rings, the sister calling back, I just let it ring.

I've had run-ins with that sister before, and do you know why? Because I didn't marry her, that's why, choosing little sister instead, oh the whole family out to lunch, trying to get in on the act, saying to me, "Well, the sister *is* older, you did seem to have your hat set for her, you two *were* engaged for four years," but what I told them, what I'd tell anyone, was that finally what it boiled down to was who it was loved cats the most, who it was had an inkling what was going on in the animal world, the animal kingdom, I told them, for by my lights that was the one true burning issue of the day and anyone worth a hill of salt would be taking sides. It was the younger one misled me on that score, put a cat in her arms in those days and she'd melt.

The *deception!* It's deception that this comes down to, that's the whole story. We've got this Neighborhood Watch, right, they're supposed to look after things, guard against thieves, against people would come in and in fifteen minutes empty your house, mostly dopers wanting your TV to prop up their habit, maybe a little Peeping Tom now and again, but generally just to watch for smoke, see nothing goes wrong, nothing irregular, that's what the Watch is for. You've got the police number by your phone, the fire department number, you note anything suspicious you're to *get on the phone*, get on it, don't waste a minute, get that baby reported, that's what the guy said when he came out and talked to us. "No," he said, "now you're not here to spy on your neighbors, poke your nose in where it's not wanted, and we sure don't want you taking the law into your own hands, none of that or you're going to be in a spot of trouble with us your own selves, so note that . . . but what you're to do is keep your eye out, your eyes open, look for strangers loitering about etc., etc., and when you see it you *get on the phone*, you got that? You call us, we'll have a squad car over practically before you hang up. That's what this program is all about, sticking together, looking out for each other, having concern for your fellow man, your fellow woman, that's it, the whole show. But *get on the phone*, you got me, that's the key, it all pays off or goes down the tube, whether or not you *man them phones* . . .

"Now we got these little stickers here . . . "

Those stickers, oh yeah, they plaster them up on their doors, they claim they're looking after you, got your best interests at heart, but when it comes down to it what I ask is did they ever get the proper spirit of the Watch? Did *anybody* ever take to the phone even *once*, excepting me?

Did they note the hawk, that's what I'm asking. Do you think a hawk is just going to fly in on its own, busy neighborhood like this? You think it wouldn't prefer to be out in the country where it's got natural business? Hawks per se, I got nothing against hawks. Live and let live.

But that hawk was brought in, I say, *brought* in, and

somebody should have taken to the phone, got that beast reported. For hawks are beasts, no doubt about it. What the book says is that the hawk is one among a bunch of diurnal birds, which means birds that belong to or appear each day, including your eagle, your vulture, your osprey, your goat-sucker, your falcon, even some gulls. What those guys do is that they fasten onto some low-life bird up in the sky and they ride those rascals down to ground, where they mangle them and do anything else they want. Or there's your chicken hawk, which is what I'm convinced this one was, and the chicken hawk, on ground or sky, it doesn't care where the prey is. What the book doesn't say much about is how these beasts got powerful feet and couldn't care less whether it's a chicken or a cat they're going after. *Prefers* a cat, if my experience is any rule. And diurnal? Forget that diurnal, these hawks go at it day *or* night, day *and* night, whenever, that is, a poor cat puts foot out of the door. There they are, scrunched up high in the branches, blinking their eyes, and here comes along a cat, there they go, zip, swoop, *gotcha*. Goodbye one squawling cat.

Where she got it, this woman down the street in her teddy underwear, is from some funny-run pet shop. Me, I never trusted any of those shops, never frequented one myself, because it has yet to be proved that they care one pinch for pets, for animals of any type, no, what they're after as is well-known is the fat profit. That's indisputable, let anybody try arguing with that. So what she does is she shoves me out into the street, practically breaks my arm, flings my kitties every which way, and that is not enough for her: she goes out to a Mafia-type pet shop and buys herself this chicken hawk, this beast groomed to kill your peaceful cat.

Okay, I was slow off the driving board, I didn't see it coming. There was the wife to contend with, what to do with her accumulating mail from various peace freak organizations, outfits I didn't even know she'd ever heard of, things like Oxfam and Women Against Porn and Adopt-a-Village. How to keep her sister off my back, what to do about the stink of clothes, how I'm to go about feeding myself, who's to take the garbage out, keep up the Watch, whether I ought to open up those rooms she'd sealed herself off in – and I tell you the sum is I'm never even noticing my old plank isn't getting much use, that the number of cats around my feed bowl is dwindling each day. A fellow in these circumstances would think *hawk?* I mean, for the first time in my life I've got all this *other stuff to worry about, a thousand letters to the wife all saying We thank you for your support, insane* stuff, and frankly what I find myself saying to myself is Brother, I don't see how a person can live this way. Not that I want to open up a sewer, but that's pretty much how I was feeling over that period, like I was down in it, like as if the *whole* neighborhood, the whole *nation* was conspiring against me, putting the screws to me, just the way a cornered cat might feel or your nose could scent the food but you don't even know where the bowl is anymore.

So the cats were down to *three,* plus my kitties which I thank God I was keeping inside, before I even *noticed.* Three! Now that meant maybe *thirty* wiped off the face of this earth, their lives just short-circuited, *gone!* What I did at first was think of my wife's *mass grave* idea, and blame her, think maybe she was behind it all, she and her sister and could be the *entire* family. So I get on the phone, meaning to lay down the law to her, tell her I'm getting the whole Animal Welfare arm of the government on this case, but it turns out I'm not even talking to her, it's some fruitcake I've got on the line, some weird old geezer occupying their place, some distant relative the sister has rented the place to, and all he knows is the sister and another woman, the one was with her, have packed up and moved to, he thinks, Montana for six months, six months or six years, ever how long it takes them to sort out their lives, he says, and put it back together.

"Montana!" I say. "Jesus Christ, who would want to go to Montana?"

But he's calm, he's saying Montana is all right, nothing wrong with Montana, he's practically recommending the place, and just yaks-yaks so I can hardly get a word in, and by this time I'm looking over to my open window where the plank is and only two of my cats are around the bowl now and, goddamn, they look like they've been through the washer, the fur half-gone on their backs and this crazed fearful look in their eyes, the two of them so tame and crippled now I can actually walk over and pet them with not once getting a finger bitten or their claws raking all over me.

So I've abandoned the phone and I'm there bent at the window, looking out of it at tree, earth and sky, asking the two cats where the third one has got to, when I feel this shadow fall over my neck, and you know exactly what it was, I look up and there's this chicken hawk in a dive at the very window, at my head, if you please, no doubt thinking in its ignorance I am some kind of new disembodied *cat*. The truth, and I tell you I pulled in my head just in time.

It swoops on, away into the trees, pulling in those terrible feet, and I'm there blinking, can't believe my eyes, asking myself, What has happened to this neighborhood? What has gone wrong, how mean the change in a world that once had values, had kept its nose to the wheel, could separate burning issue from the rabble's false flame.

That's it, that's it exactly, I felt I'd suddenly waked up and found the world no longer as I had left it.

I even went to the phone, hung up on this geezer who was still on the line, talking about Montana, and I called the SPCA if only to see if they still existed. To see had the world changed that much.

Too dumbfounded with grief, too overrun with melancholy and *perplexia*, with the awful truth, even to report that hawk.

Yes, that's how bad it was.

You see that space up there? That space up there means a lot of time went by while I was sorting things out, putting my life back together. What that space means too is that you don't have to go to Montana. What I figured out, and figured out fast or that space would be a lot bigger, was the teddy woman's part in it. She'd gone to that pet store. She'd bought that hawk. Her aim being simple: to clear the neighborhood of all pets, particularly cats, particularly mine.

So it's night now. That night I went down to her place. I could see her in there behind her closed curtains: her veiled figure. Up close, at kneel between the ferns, I could hear her talking in a low voice: "Come here. Now go there." That's what she was saying. And whenever she spoke I could see this great hawk shape hulk up above her, see the great sprawl of wings, and behind her the massive shadow these wings made on her wall. "Come here. Yes. Good, oh do more of that." That kind of talk. And always just after she'd spoken, this colossal hulking, this beating of wings, the flapping shadows on her wall. And my heart swole up in fright for myself, for the whole of the neighborhood. It swole up in terror for my own and our time here. If the

Watch couldn't keep this out, what could? What next? I shut my eyes and my heart closed up, though I still could hear her: "That nice. I like that. Let's have more of that." I could see it all with my eyes closed, the big swoop, the powerful dive, the terrible feet gripping my backside, my flesh tearing, the hawk lifting me up, carrying me to some far, awful place where it would rip me open, rend my guts, drink my blood – but what happened is he got me up about so high and his strength gave out, I was too heavy even for him, so I crashed through that woman's window, was just let go, and it just so happened that she was standing there, her back to the glass, not so much as her teddy on this time, her just screaming, me with my skin ripped open, the blood all over, trying to extricate myself from her wriggling body, catching in the interim only a glimpse of the goddamn hawk as it swooped out of the door.

I Want to Know the Answer

I had with me this woman. I said, Are you prepared to accept sexual fidelity to me until we can be together in paradise? She didn't answer right away. She wanted to think about it. I didn't mind that. I'd taken a long time to arrange this question in my mind before I asked it of her. Things took time. I knew that. I'd taken the time and still the question had not come out the way I'd arranged it. One thing I knew was that I had to have her answer before I left her on this street corner, before I left this town this evening. I had to leave town this evening, there was no taking time about that.

Will you be sexually faithful to me until we can be together in paradise? That's what I had meant to ask. How I meant to say it. So I said it again, I grabbed her arm and I said it. Will you? She was walking a little faster now and I had to take a stride or two to get myself abreast of her and I had to grab her arm. Will you? Her head whipped over at me, her head whipped back, she tried to free that arm. She looked like a shaggy dog to me in that second, in that instant when her eyes were confronting mine. Like a shag rug, a piece cut out, piece from the floor you and maybe a hundred others, say a family of four, had walked on, trod on, for forty or fifty years, never a cleaning; then a little piece cut out and maybe flapped a few times to shake out the sticks, the big stuff, and then fitted up over her naked head so she'd look human. A brown carpet, filthy, I said that. Anyway, that's how she looked, not nice, not nice, not the least bit nice, not in that second. She was nice, but not in that second. She didn't look like anyone who would ever be sexually faithful. I saw that in the second her head turned. When I was a boy – but wait, I'm not falling into that trap, not in that "when I was" trap. That trap – you're walking along, I'm walking along, and I can see that "when I was" trap in front of me before my foot steps down, the same way Tarzan could see a pool of quicksand. Quicksand. Tarzan could always see, he was always aware of, where the quicksand was. If it was anywhere in his jungle, in his jungle, he knew it. Snakes were different. Snakes were the one thing different in the jungle. In the jungle they'd drop down on you from a tree, on Tarzan, I mean, from a tree. And you saw it coming, you always did, but Tarzan never. Tarzan never. He had a blind side, but you yourself, you didn't have this particular blind side. No, you didn't. You were A-okay on the snakes and the blind-side question. My mom now, Mom now, she was all blind side. In a jungle she wouldn't have lasted a minute. The snakes would have eaten her alive. You know what I mean. Quicksand, okay, snakes not okay, they'd squeeze her to death in a minute. So I asked her, this one, I asked her – I was within my right and I asked her – How do you feel about sexual congress? We've done that, we've had that – but how do you feel about sexual fidelity? Now, that's one that will get you, it will drop down on you from a tree and squeeze out your breath in a minute. I knew this. I was born knowing this. I only had to look at my mother. You come to life chained to your mother's bed. You do, but that is not what I am saying. Okay, reconsider, maybe it is. You're chained to that bed, but you're chained there by the snake, that's what I mean, and I don't mean the snake you may think I mean, I mean the snake that always went after Tarzan. That's how they do it. And they don't use that snake from the Tarzan movie either, because you can see that snake coming before Tarzan can. It's a particular kind of snake, this one, you can't see it. But it's got you shackled. You can feel it squeezing your bones.

Once, I was in bed, I was about nine years old, in this bed, my mother's bed, I was down at the foot of the bed, across the bed, and my father and mother were in the bed, too. They were in the bed the other way, the right way, and I was at the foot of the bed and I heard her say, Don't wake him. You better not wake him. I ought not to let you do this, don't do this. Don't do it. She was whispering but I heard her, although at that time, at that time, I didn't know it was my father she was saying this to because at this time I didn't know it was my father in this bed. All I knew is that I was at the foot of the bed, the wrong way in the bed, and that two other people were in the bed. My head was under the covers, a cold night, a freezing night, and I could smell their feet. Feet, that's all, that's all I smelled.

I shouldn't let you do this, that's what she said. I didn't hear him say anything. I never heard him say anything. The whole time he didn't say anything and I was listening, I want to tell you I was listening, I was still as a bullet and listening. But my father never said anything, not one word. He rolled up over her, you see, and the mattress shook, the mattress shivered, and she said, You better not wake him. It was too late, wasn't I listening? Wasn't I smelling their feet? Wasn't I? I was. He didn't say anything. Not one word. He never had. I thought to myself, Why is he here? Where did he come in from? Who is he, anyway? And the mattress went on shaking. It went on forever shaking. His feet kept poking me. Both his feet kept poking me. The cold bottoms of his feet, poke, poke. He had his feet against me because I was his brace. He was using me as his brace as he did this with my mother, and what was happening was I was being shoved right down between the foot of the mattress and the heel of the bed frame. There was a space there, a hole, and he was shoving his feet against me and that's where I was going, into that hole. She kept saying, "Shhh," that's what she kept saying. "Shhh, don't wake him, I'm a fool to let you be doing this," that's what she kept saying.

"You'll be gone in the morning, you better be gone in the morning," yes, she said that.

It went on forever. It did, it was forever, don't tell me it wasn't. You'd see those people in the Tarzan movie stepping off into the quicksand, running into the quicksand, you'd see their shoulders, then only the head, their eyes, and what would you see next? A hat up there on top of the bubbling sand. Then not even the hat. That's what you would see. That's what I would see, and you too, if we went to the same movie. All my friends, we saw the same movie, we'd come out into the sunlight and we'd say, "Did you see that hat? Did you see that hat? Boy, I'm staying away from quicksand," that's what we'd say. "Quicksand's not going to get me."

"Shhh, don't wake him."

What I'm saying is, Where'd he come from? He hadn't been around in years and years. He never said anything. Never. He just put his feet against me and pushed. There were these covers, these heavy covers, I told you that. The feet. You had to have all these covers, the freezing cold, so my head is under there.

I don't know what I was doing in her bed in the first place. I had my own bed, but I guess what happened is – wait now, this is how it was. I had my bed and then he'd come home, he'd come back, out of the blue, my father had, he'd just knocked on the door and come on in, come on up those stairs and sat down and somehow he'd got my bed. That's right, he had to have my bed because she wasn't having him in her bed, that's one possible way it happened, but why it was I was down at the foot of the bed, across the bed, you'll just have to make up your own explanation for that. His feet were all over me. That's what I hated worse, his feet, all that pushing.

"I shouldn't let you," I hated that, too.

Grit your teeth. That's what you do. That's what I was doing, gritting my teeth, the same as I was doing when I said to her this sexual fidelity question. Paradise matters. You want to get there, you have to ask it. Will you be sexually faithful to me until we can reach paradise? I've told you, she wanted to think about this. She didn't want to answer right away. And I wasn't rushing her. Let her grit her teeth while she thinks about it. Let her think she can run. It isn't the right question, that's what she was saying to herself. I bet you a dollar that was it. I better watch this guy, that's what she was saying. There we were, out in the night, we've settled on the price, we've established that, we've done it to everyone's satisfaction, done it *as agreed*, and here comes along this question out of the blue. Fifty dollars, you think I ever meant her to keep that fifty dollars? You're crazy. I don't deal in that kind of craziness. She keeps it, she answers the question. It's that simple. I can see quicksand coming, see that hat, and I don't deal in either. I don't deal in hats. Hats are fuck-all, that's how I feel about hats. Paradise, that's another question. Paradise, now that I think of it, is the *only* question. There is no other question. In the whole of the universe. You can be down under the covers, under a thousand blankets, under quicksand, and that's the question. Where's paradise? Where's sexual fidelity, too? Okay, that's another one. Maybe there are more questions, after all. I don't care how many questions there are. Questions, any you can think of, can go the way of that hat. They can go right down. They can go down where you never see them because they came to you so long ago, and were answered so long ago, that now it's as if you've come out of the movie and you're standing around with your friends, asking these things, but what you're really saying is, What can we do now? We've seen the movie, what can we do now? Go back home? Are you kidding? You're wanting me to go back home? You're crazy.

Okay, so after some years what you find yourself thinking about as you leave the movie is sexual favors. She doesn't look cheap. No, they've never looked cheap, not to me. What they look like is that they are going to cost you your life. They are going to cost you the whole of it. One way or another. I don't care about the fifty dollars, what's fifty dollars, fifty dollars is nothing in the grand scheme of the universe, it's zilch and nothing when it comes to the final payoff. We've agreed on the final payoff, and fifty dollars is nothing, not even if you've got to have it up front. "Up front, baby, or I don't move," that's what this one said. "I don't move from this corner." We've both been around, we've got no argument. To hell with fifty dollars, I say, I say that, but what I say too, pretty soon, after we've done it, after we've done it *in the manner agreed* and in accordance with the purchase price, is, What next? What do we do next? What do I do? You can't go home. You can't get into paradise. Not right away, so what do you do?

You ask for something. It seems to me it isn't asking too much to expect a little sexual fidelity before or until you get there. That's what I mean. That's what I'm saying. So you put the question to her. *I – me – I – I* put the question to her because I know you wouldn't. You can never be counted on to put the question to her, whereas I don't mind doing it. I do it for you, I'm accustomed. "Can I expect you to be faithful to me until we reach paradise?" There is only one question and that's it, that's the one, and it's what we are all wanting to know.

Okay, she grits her teeth.

She yanks that arm.

She's thinking it over. She didn't see it coming, there's this weirdo beside her, maybe he's got this knife at her throat and maybe he hasn't, but the answer better be the right one, that's what I'm saying. It better be, because I'm not here to hurt. I'm not here to inflict pain or cause trouble. It's just that I want to know. I want to know the answer.

Help me.

Blues Roots or
You Tear Me Apart

This is what Bovine's lover or mistress or girlfriend says to him.

"You're tearing me to pieces," she says.

She says this to him over and over.

Bovine has brought an old John Henry Barbee blues record over to her place.

"Let's put on John Henry," he says.

"I wish you wouldn't," she says. "What kind of name is Bovine anyhow?"

She's been crying all day. She's been in her bathroom, crying, and in her bed, crying, and at the shoppette when she went out for crackers and cheese. The only time today she hasn't been crying was when she was on the phone talking to a distant son. This, to her mind, is strange, because that boy, over the years, has made her cry more than anyone.

She's not crying now. She stopped crying the minute Bovine came through the door.

"I'll pour us a *tonique*," she says.

Bovine doesn't know what kind of name Bovine is, and at the moment has this at the bottom of his list of troubles.

"Turn up the Barbee," he says.

To the woman, mixing drinks, this remark, for reasons

that she can perfectly comprehend, smacks her as a kind of rueful baby-talk.

She can feel her eyes moistening, and wishes she could stop these thoughts: *Turn up the Barbee! Turn up the* BAY-BEE! *The* BAR-BEE *has turned up, and is talking baby-talk.* All the men in her life, she reflects, at one time or another talk baby-talk. She wonders what it is in her that brings out this trait in them. She wonders how it is other women escape this humiliation. Perhaps they don't.

"Turn it up yourself," she says.

She once was with a man who never talked at all or brought over morbid records to her place, and she finds herself, these days, thinking more and more of him.

She supposes this is why she has had such a flood of tears today.

Or maybe it is because it had been so long since her son called.

Or it could be nothing more than her acute awareness of a vacancy in her life, and the knowledge that such condition is likely to continue for a long, long time.

"You're tearing me apart," she says to Bovine, yet again.

She says it to him this time with a soft, apologetic smile, because she can see that Bovine is absolutely lost when he hears such words. Bovine does not know what he could do differently, short of leaving his wife.

He is a little proud, too, to see that he has such power over her emotions. He is a little proud, and a little ashamed, and definitely confused. She can see this in his face when she says, "You are tearing me apart," and this is one reason she says it to him, over and over.

For the moment, Bovine is untroubled. Barbee and the blues have got him. He is humming along softly, with the Barbee tune, and plunking an imaginary guitar.

He looks, to the woman's mind, like a total imbecile, which it gives her considerable pleasure to acknowledge.

"Here is your *tonique*," she says.

She remembers that the man who never spoke, this man in her past, her son's father, never even spoke in restaurants. She had to order for him.

Bovine, his eyes closed, is snapping his fingers, humming, and bobbing his head.

He is a man who dearly loves his blues.

"He will have *scampi*," she would tell the waiter.

"He will have a Pilsner Urquell, and bring a toothpick, would you please?"

He was always picking his teeth, that one was.

The woman, sipping her *tonique*, sitting in a chair across from Bovine and steadily watching him, finds herself smiling, as she remembers this silent man. If she can but put her mind to it, she will remember every dish that ever was put before him.

"He'll have squid," she'd say.

"He'll have beef-with-watercress-pie à la mode."

"He'll have the same as I and my son are having."

The silent man's one virtue was that he ate hungrily whatever was put before him.

Bovine is now standing, his legs apart, his body gyrating along with the blues song.

Watching this man's joy, the woman feels some rejuvenation. She feels sprightly and frolicsome, and wants more than anything to dance. All her troubles would vanish, if only she could dance.

"Let's go out," she says. "Let's get plastered."

Bovine groans. "Oh, God," says Bovine. "Can't I listen to my friend Barbee, in peace?"

The woman has been dancing over the carpet in front of him, swishing her skirt. Now she sags down.

"You are tearing me to pieces," she says.

Bovine reaches over and increases the volume of his Barbee. Walls, ceiling, and floor are now vibrating. Neighbors in this apartment building will be clapping hands over their ears.

The woman can hardly remember the silent man's name. Sixteen months with him, her son's father, and now she can hardly dredge it up. His *pet* name; it is the pet name his family had for him, that is now eluding her.

"There is a new place around the corner," she tells Bovine. "Informal. We wouldn't even have to change."

Bovine shakes his head. That shake means he can not hear a word she's saying.

"You are tearing me to pieces," she says. She says this with a big smile. She loves saying this to him, smiling, knowing he's deaf to every word.

"I absolutely adore you," she says. "I want you to hurry home this minute, and murder your wife. I want you to bring me one million unmarked dollars in a briefcase, and to tell me you are willing to die for me a thousand times because your love for me knows no bounds."

She hoots with laughter. She is having a wonderful time, and her *tonique* is now empty. She has rarely seen a glass so empty as her glass is.

Bovine is happy, too. He wiggles his hips, he beams. He says, "I didn't know you were so fond of the blues."

The woman refreshes her drink. She pours the gin deep.

She wonders if she *ever* knew the silent man's pet name. It might be that this name never existed and she is thinking of someone else, or of the secret names her son had for one or another of his little friends.

He was silent, she remembers that, but he was a good listener. He *absorbed* all that one said or did.

He never received any mail, she remembers that.

"I am bored," she tells Bovine. "You never want to go out with me anywhere."

When the side is done Bovine gets up and turns the record over. "Oh dem blues," he says. "Oh dat Barbee, he ain't gonna pick no mo cotton, no he ain't. We ain't never, any one of us, gonna pick no mo cotton, hallelujah! How he does it, gets that sound," says Bovine, "is with a knife blade or Coke bottle up around the guitar neck. He's a killer, with that bottle."

The woman composes herself. This *tonique* is pure gin, and now that she has poured it, she is out of the mood. The silent man, unlike Bovine, had a drinking problem. First he had it, and then they both had it, and one thing led to the other, and what this led to was the beginning of the end. She can't recall the pet name she had for him, but nearly everything else about the silent man is clear.

He was into astronomy, she remembers that.

He was in deep watch, nightly from their rooftop, of the heavens.

He loved the heavens, she suspected, because these heavens were as silent as himself, and a similar riddle.

Bovine is now again strumming away with Barbee, mouthing the words.

When this one leaves, when Bovine leaves, the woman decides, she will go out and have herself a quiet, candle-light dinner. She will have this dinner by herself, and not talk to anyone.

Bovine turns down the volume.

"Listen to this one," he says. "I got a little wife, she ain't but 'lev'n years old . . . "

She and her husband and their infant son would sit up on the rooftop, of nights, studying the heavens for alien movement. For shooting stars. She could close her eyes now, and feel the nursing baby against her skin, as she had felt it then. The stars dropping and burning out, one after the other.

"But her mama," Bovine sings, "sev'nteen, was purest gold."

Bovine whoops his laughter. "Yea, doggy!" he says. "Oh dem Barbee blues, they tear me to pieces. Barbee wasn't his real name, you know. No, old Barbee shot a white man was triflin' with his woman, and he headed off into the swamps. Into alligator country. Practically wasn't heard from for another thirty years."

The woman, who knows the blues as well as the next person, knows that this is only *one* side of the story.

"That was nice," she says, as the record ends.

Bovine sits as though in misery, his shoulders slumped, clearly wishing he could play this record a second time.

But the woman is holding his coat.

She has poured her *tonique* down the sink, and is standing clear-eyed, waiting, at her door.

"Chasing me away, huh?"

At last Bovine is putting on his shoes. He is at last putting on his coat.

He kisses her, his arms around her, hers limp at her side.

"God, that was nice," he says. "I can never listen to the blues at home. Too repetitive. Monotonous. Too much the man bitchin' about what's done to *him*. Only two kinds of women in a blues song. An image thing."

He is clutching this precious record to his bosom. His eyes are wet and it looks as though any minute he might burst into tears.

But the woman, observing this, wouldn't go out on a limb. No, she wouldn't go out on a limb.

176

Or onto *an image thing.*

After Bovine has gone she remains by the door, scanning the room, conscious of its silence. Her breath drawn.

It is like an actual *creature,* this silence is.

It comes to her, after a minute, that it is a creature without guile. Meaning no harm.

"Honey," she says, laughing. "You tear me up."

Even so, she stands so for some little while, hands up over her face, undecided what she will next do.

She does not care what music Bovine listens to, or doesn't listen to, at home.

He can jump out of a window, Bovine can.

Thirty years lost in the swamp. Now that is something to think about.

She fluffs pillows, clears away crackers and cheese, she washes up.

She throws herself into bed.

Precious *relief,* she thinks.

"I have not the least smidgen of regret," she says. "High time I shucked Bovine and *all* of them." She keens a brief laughter, for in truth they are not that many. And they are all, except for Bovine, scattered – as is her son – to the ends of the earth.

She stares at the ceiling, unable to free her thoughts.

She sees Barbee in his swamp, combating his crocodiles.

Swatting gnats, mosquitoes, steering through legion upon legion of dead trees.

Thinking: thirty more years.

It is night now in the swamp, and she sees him – sees herself – oaring blindly, endlessly, through black and sinister water.

As she did today during her crying spell – before Bovine's arrival, before her son's call: *Just thinking of you, Mom. Just wishing you heart's cheer.*

That haunting, screechy, nerve-tearing sound you get with knife blade or bottle high on the neck: it is worth enduring the blues, to get that sound. It is so much like what goes on inside the heart.

Covici's Guilt

This is what Covici says to himself; it is how he talks: "When you do a thing that's wrong, that everyone knows is wrong, why can't you admit to yourself that what you have done is wrong? Even a little bit."

Covici does not reply to this. Covici is underground. When Covici is underground, and walking, as he is now, he can make no headway against these troublesome queries.

This is what Covici next asks himself: "Why, if what I have done is wrong, do they not point out to me the crime, or crimes, I have committed, with the full specifics, and perhaps, even, with the hint of full forgiveness, once I have consented to and apologized for my array of misdeeds?"

"However gross," he then added. "What a person needs are conditional alternatives. Everything spelled out."

Yes, that was the trouble. If his enemies, or those whom he had wounded or offended, offered alternatives conditional on clear-cut demonstrations of self-reproach, and a promise – a guarantee – to forever alter his miserable patterns of behavior, then a person – even a person of Covici's limited achievements – could perhaps make amends. Could even redeem himself.

Covici walked. He did not care where he walked or how long. He would walk all night, if necessary.

This is what he thought: Walking mellows a fellow.
Clears the head.

Walking, you come to see things about yourself you wouldn't ordinarily see.

In *their* shoes, he told himself, he would express a little sympathy. He'd show a certain tolerance.

It wasn't as if he'd bombed Hiroshima, or murdered the Sister – what was her name? – that nun who fed and clothed the poor.

Like that, just that easily, Covici emerged into light. It was raining, he noticed the rain, but even so he felt buoyant.

What a relief, he thought, after being so long underground. Walking in the dark.

It's depressing, he thought. I depress myself.

An idea came to him, and he went in search of a public telephone.

The voice that answered was not one he recognized, nor did the party appear to know his voice. The party said: "Who is this? What do you want?"

Covici summoned his thoughts. He would give a false name.

This is what Covici said: "I am calling about Covici. I understand he has committed a dastardly act, and I want to be sure something is being done about it. He must not be allowed to wiggle off the hook this time."

The voice, cautious now, asked what business it was of his.

This is how Covici replied: "The man's a scoundrel. He's treated me abominably. Yes, and never a word of apology or regret. He deserves whatever bad tidings come his way, wouldn't you say? We can not let this man continue trodding over everyone. Don't you agree?"

For some seconds the voice didn't respond. Then Covici heard a soft click, and the phone was dead.

So Covici took another of his long walks underground.

You get no *help*, he told himself.

You'd think we all lived in *caves*.

Later, Covici decided to call his wife. It was entirely possible that she might be glad to hear from him.

The phone rang for a long time, and finally Charlotte's voice was on the line.

He said hello, and gave her the same false name he'd given the earlier party.

"Covici," she instantly said. "Why are you pretending to be someone else? It's loathsome and ridiculous, these end-less impersonations. What have you done this time? What now? No, don't tell me."

Before he could stop himself, Covici was babbling out something about his innocence. The unfairness of people. The constant stream of unjust and scurrilous accusations that came his way. He was asking Charlotte why it was that in every situation people seemed to think, or expect, the worst of him?

His wife had been trying to interrupt. Now he heard her say: "You are a pest, Covici. You are a bore. No one hates you, no, it's just that we cry with fatigue at the very thought of you, and would weep with gratitude if we never again heard your name. Stop calling us. Leave us alone. For ten years you have been plaguing us with this show of grief and guilt and we are all fed up with it. Including your children. Forget it, would you? Can't you? I beg you. *Please*, Covici. Please?"

Covici had the feeling that he'd arrived at some impor-tant breakthrough. He saw glimmers of light.

Excitedly, he said, "Ten years ago? What was it I did ten

years ago? That makes you all hate me? Don't spare me. Tell me every detail."

With that remark, this line, too, went dead.

Covici stood in the pooled rain, in sinking light, watching the wetness climb his trouser leg.

This is what he said: "They will go on stabbing knives into my back until I am dead. They will never be satisfied. I have simply got to accept that they are not nice people – not nice at all – and go my merry way."

But even as he said this, he was digging into his pocket for another coin. He was already dialing.

"That chap, Covici," he said to the answering party. "Do you know what he's done now? Have you any idea what that imbecile has been up to? I for one will never forgive him this time! *Never!* I have come to the end of my rope."

Smoke

The doctor said can we cut him, which I thought was reasonable. We stood by, waiting for my mother to answer. Brad, my brother, was there, and the doctor, and we waited for my mother to answer. She waited, too, and with her the answer had to come from a long way down. It had to come from her whole life, down.

This is for science, folks. To my mind that is what the doctor was saying. But to her mind it was gross what this doctor was suggesting. Can we cut him? Here was a guy who had been a hard case all his life, but now it finally came to this: he could help out. His organs for science. An eye for an eye, a tooth for a tooth.

"What do you think, Mom?"

She was looking hurt. She was also looking furious.

"Do you want to sit down?" my brother asked.

"Son of a bitch," she said.

That's what she said. She wouldn't sit, she wasn't pacing either. All she was doing was staring hard into our faces and the doctor's face. We were all her enemies.

"Son of a bitch, no, I do not want to sit down."

Then she looked at her husband. He was already turning yellow. He had already gone where the dead go – and they go somewhere, something goes somewhere, I think we can say that much. If something is there, then isn't, then you can say that much. You could see it in his body, what had gone, though his corpse still had that peculiar swelling. That bloated look. She looked at him and I guess what she saw was his body cut.

Dissected.

In pieces.

My brother and I looked at him, too, and maybe we are having what you call second thoughts.

"Now, Mom," my brother says. "I really think you ought to sit down."

"Would you shut the fuck up about sitting down," she says.

These are quite the words, coming from her, who does not use such words.

"All right," my brother says. "Then, goddamn it, I will sit down."

He does not either. He does not normally use such words.

So because I don't want my brother to feel he's alone in this I take the chair beside him, which just leaves the doctor and our mother standing.

"I realize your confusion," the doctor says.

She pushes his shoulder. She shoots up a hand and shoves him away.

"I am not confused," she says. "And you can go fuck yourself if you think I need to sit down."

My brother walks away. He walks up the hall, and I know what he is thinking. He is thinking, You can not help this woman. You can not help her. You offer a helping hand to this woman and she will break your fingers.

The doctor has this pad in his hand and he studies the pad. He is a doctor in no hurry. He is not a doctor who minds the hard way my mother looks at him. She is not his mother.

"Assholes," my mother says, and she kicks the chair she won't sit on.

"Give me a cigarette," she says to me.

The doctor shakes his head.

I light her cigarette and she smokes it here in this hall where you are not supposed to smoke, and no one raises an objection.

She wishes someone would. It is plain to see that she wishes someone would, so she can tell them what they can do with themselves.

She goes over to where he is dead on the bed, under a white sheet folded at his chin, and she blows smoke over his face.

"He looks sweet," she says. "He looks perfectly natural."

My brother and I look at each other and my brother says, "We'd better shake a leg, Mom."

The doctor concurs. He's in no hurry, but he's in a hurry that much.

I go over and hook an arm around her waist.

"What's your decision, Mom?"

"Put this out," she says.

And I take her cigarette and look about for a place I can put it.

"It was not his liver," she says. "His liver had not a goddamn thing to do with it."

This she says to the doctor.

What the doctor says is, If we performed an autopsy, we might have a better – . He stops there. He's seen her face.

"Cut him?" she says.

My brother and I sit down and hold hands like little children.

She says to the doctor, "Keep him on that bed until I get a hearse here to take him home."

She says to the doctor, "I wouldn't let you cut my cat."

She says to us, "Let me sit down," and my brother and I jump aside and help her sit.

"You," she tells the doctor. "You can go. Go kill someone else."

The doctor goes. He is not a bad doctor, but he is a doctor whose luck today has been bad.

Our mother takes my hands and my brother's hands and she holds them on her lap.

"Okay," she says. "Let's shake that leg."

But we stay on there with her as she looks at him.

"Light me another one," she says.

All of us light up.

She looks at him, we look at her.

"Don't speak," she says. "Don't breathe a word."

We don't. We do exactly as she says.

Body Count

These people died, and in short order, it seems to me, although when I put my mind to it and rehash their departures, lining up the days, I can see that these deaths cover a good many years, if one views them strictly by calendar time. But I am not inclined to look at the matter in this way, and one death falls upon the heels of the other as steadfastly as the fence posts strung upon the very roadway by which I arrived at this place twelve years ago.

A March day that was, windy and cold.

It concerns me, the sheer number of those who have died, and that I am shortly to join them, as are others here, concerns me too. There is a cornfield across the way, which those of us in the north wing may look out upon from our rooms, and I am reminded that it was from just such a field, as a small girl peering through the growth, that I witnessed my grandmother's death.

They had been boiling water in two large, black-iron pots, I recall, and in the first of these they scalded a pig, and afterwards my grandfather and some of his sons hung and gutted it. In the second pot, through the night and on into the morning of the day of her funeral, they were cooking up a stew of some kind, Brunswick stew, it must have been, for there were a good many people to feed.

This was in 1944, with the war underway.

She was a hard woman, to my mind my grandmother was, whatever else you may have heard, and her death, after all these years, has not changed my view on this, although memory of any specific harm she might have done me, or done those I most cared about, such as my brother and sister and my mother, remains vague. The curious happenstance here, which I would mention, is that my grandfather, who survived my grandmother by some three decades, never once in my presence or in the presence of anyone else that I know – and let us say I would know – mentioned her name or spoke of her absence during all of those thirty years he survived her. He spoke of an absence in his life, but did not give that absence her name. Which is what leaves me to believe what I believe about that, which is that it was easier for him this way, although harder on others. On my mother, for instance, who, as she aged, was inclined to look back upon those days when she – or another woman in her skin – might have made sounder choices about her life. She would have found it useful, I mean to say, to talk to him about those choices her own mother made, for comparisons have a place in the scheme of things.

Grandmother died in the side yard, while throwing feed to the chickens, and I saw that, too, saw her fall, and try, on her belly, to scratch her way to the back door, as the chickens fluttered by, attempting to peck feed from her hands.

My grandfather, who was called in from the fields, took her in his arms and laid her out on the featherbed in the living room where they slept. I recall someone saying, "Take off her shoes," and someone did take them off, although after a few minutes my grandfather, who had been studying her dead form from his rocking chair, got up and dusted them and put them back on her feet. Later on, he walked alone across the fields and informed neighbors, which took until dark, and that night he went out and selected the pig.

It was wartime, as I said, with food in short supply, and people did not kill their pigs with equanimity, so I interpret this decision as an indication of the high regard he felt for her.

I observed her burial – hidden in the corn, alone, playing pattycake in the mud – and the people afterwards, through the afternoon, ate the stew, together with other foods which they had brought themselves. The men ate theirs mostly sitting on the top rail of a high fence. The women sat on logs and lard cans and on the tailgates of trucks, swinging their legs, making, on the whole, a much bigger fuss about all the things they found to do. My mother was there, too, though I only saw her four times. Once was when she stood on the hill, by the grave, the prettiest woman there, with the sun revealing her legs under her dress. A second time was when she stood talking to some women seated in one of the trucks, and a third time was near dark, when she went with three men to the side of the barn, away from everyone's view, and shared a drink with them. When it came her turn, she wiped the mouth of the bottle with her skirt, and I remember the men thought that amusing.

The fourth time was in the cornfield. I got careless and she must have spotted me, because when I looked up she was coming towards me through the corn rows, reciting the pattycake rhyme.

"Come and eat," she said. "I'll bet you haven't eaten anything all day, except these pattycakes. Are they good?" She wiped my face with the back of her hand and said, "You are filthy as pie." I told her I had seen her showing off her legs, wondering if this would make her angry, but she only smiled, and said my pattycakes had gone a bit dry. Didn't I need more water?

"Did they cover up her coffin yet?"

"I don't know," she said. "Maybe they are waiting to see how many of us will jump into it."

My grandmother was wearing, on the day she keeled over, as she wore every other day, a black, cotton dress, which came to her heels, and black shoes, her hair in a tight bun on her head. Pictures I have seen of her in a white-lined casket show her with her hair down, though I never saw her this way while she was alive, and would not have recognized her, had not others in the family told me who she was. This, although I lived in that house for six years as a child. In the corn that day, I did not see her at all, only the few dozen who were mourning her, which was not something I was doing, that day in the corn.

From my place in the corn, as the people were eating, I heard any number of them repeat the story of how she died, and the adulatory manner in which they claimed her chickens always did "all but eat from her hand," which story lent her a special dispensation I, and my brother and sister, and perhaps my mother as well, did not think she deserved.

Why my mother passed that remark about other people jumping into the grave before they could fill it up is something I have often thought about, although a good many people around here whom I have told this story to give the impression that they know exactly what she meant.

"You are an innocent," Sarah Abernathy has told me. "Unless you are keeping something from us, you have been spared the awful depths those of us older than you know to our core."

This, it seems to me, is itself a strange observation, since I am old as Methuselah myself.

"Why don't you spit it out," Sarah said. "Whatever it is."

My grandfather sired – if I may use that ridiculous word – five sons and eight daughters, and some of them died, too, before my grandmother died that day with the chickens pecking in the yard. They died at birth and there is much to be said about that, and I expect I will.

But before my grandmother's death there was their oldest son who perished, in the war, in a prison camp, I believe it was, in Germany, in 1944, some months before peace was declared and before the newspapers began filling their pages with reports of Nazi horrors against the Jews. He would have been my uncle, although I did not think of him as an uncle, and for reasons peculiar to my own way of thinking, his is not a death that counts significantly in my mind. His death counts in the accumulated totals, but it was a vague, far-off death that will have meaning on some other person's ledger – his wife's, for instance – rather than on mine. Now, of course, she also is dead. I have ticks by both their names, but have recorded no details, preferring to restrict my account to those who perished on familiar, or home, soil.

There were three in my grandmother's family, if memory serves me, who died at birth. This being, though, not a thing I want yet to dwell on, since if my reading into the history of the period – that time and that place, not to mention other places and times where similar misfortunes and atrocities were occurring – is not unique and in fact it was rather to be expected, I believe. Basing this solely on what I have read of same, or heard about first-hand, three deaths at birth in a rural family numbering thirteen sons and daughters, where existence was marginal at best, is not uncommon. For this region and for that time. Which is where I would let that matter rest, if you want to know the truth, there being very little we can do about it now, and less, I suppose, that could have been done about it then, without there had occurred a total restructuring of the social order. Or perhaps not even then. Because if it could have been done, would it not have been done? This is the point to be made about that. Or at any rate it is the point that others – notably counselors and attendants here who suggest we should be content sucking our thumbs – have made within my hearing, and to my distaste, for my own views on the matter are that all of those who governed us, who declared or interpreted our laws and set our public policies, should have been struck dumb and blinded on the spot, and their heirs and legatees as well.

Because, according to my computations, and conceding my lean ability with mathematics, but taking a typical year – say, 1914 – this is the figure, rounded off, I have come up with. Seven thousand were born dead, or died within minutes of their delivery from the womb. Roughly, yes, seven thousand. In any of these given years, in this vicinity alone. Within a radius, let us say, of one hundred miles. That is what I figure. Including, of course, mothers who, for whatever reasons, did not survive the ordeal.

Or young unwed girls who fell under the knife.

Yes, that is what I have come up with. That is what my exploratory research, my research to date, reveals, and I would be surprised to find I was very far off, despite the absence of extensive resource materials in this place where I have been obliged to finish out my days.

In this institution alone, hundreds of such deaths have been verified. *Hundreds!*

"Spit it out," Sarah Abernathy told these women, and they spat.

Official documents, I am sure, paint a prettier picture.

But real life, the "facts" acknowledged by living witnesses to these deaths, to my mind are more to be trusted.

Whispered testimony, word-of-mouth, the odd slip made during innocent conversation, is by no means to be discounted.

My son, the one who troubled himself to ask, on one of his rare visits said, "Mother, how have you arrived at this figure? Seven thousand sounds unlikely, considering the sparsity of population in this region."

"Listen to people," I told him. "Look around. You might even ask, 'why sparse?'"

"I wish you'd forget this infant mortality business," he said. "Think happy thoughts."

"There are no happy thoughts," I told him. Yet even as I said this, I felt happy, because he had come to see me and was making such a show of his affection.

When I was more robust than I am now, and more diligently in pursuit of the truth, open declarations, whispered hints, denunciations, came my way daily. Plus, there were the few books my sons presented me, before these were confiscated, and the newspaper obituaries that I could peruse when my eyesight afforded me that pleasure. Equally important in my investigation, if you want to call it that, were the files on those domiciled here over the years. Naturally enough, those lodged here have died at a brisk, all but unfathomable rate. And their files contain more information than you might think they would contain, and for a while, it may surprise you to learn, I had secret access to these files.

I gave the woman money, to let me spy. I don't mind admitting I gave her money. She would take money for other things, too – socks she had darned, that we might give our grandchildren when they visited, or little pencil sketches she made of us, caricatures, I believe they were called – before she was found out and released. But I paid her only to let me spy.

I came across a lot of useful information in these files. There were notations, for instance, often in the subject's own words, and while I might, as has been repeatedly charged, be obsessed with the matter, and possibly, from time to time, fantasize, the mentions of infanticide in these files are so numerous that I sometimes think someone was here before me, at this institution's very beginning, assembling proof:

"I lost two at birth, and never got over that."

"My sister died, giving birth, under circumstances I thought peculiar."

"I had a baby born with a blue head, who ought to have lived longer than he did."

"I lost one to what was gauged to be influenza, and another strangled in the womb."

Dr. Sarah Abernathy's statement:

"I had fourteen children. Five died at birth. *Why?*"

It is how that unfortunate woman first came to my attention. Sarah Abernathy holds the infant mortality record, among those files I perused. No one else is close. But that is only in this place. In another, this disturbing record might be surpassed.

And there is the private and secret testimony of any number of others, not all of whom, under current pressure or the tedious advances of disease, have now recanted.

Or those who in their youth, and unwed, for respectability's sake, accepted the knife.

Seven thousand, then, in this neighborhood, born dead within a single year, and I think I can say, as the pollsters do, that I am right, within a four to six percentage margin of error, nineteen times out of twenty.

Sarah Abernathy, as her body wasted away, became more and more convinced that her husband had deliberately done away with her children. He did away with them if they were sickly, and if they were girls. He would take the infants from her arms, Sarah said, and disappear with them, and five of these were dead the next time she saw them. If she saw them again at all.

Indeed, I am given to fantasizing, and often these days, gazing from the window of my room, entranced, see myself as a little girl playing pattycake in the distant corn; I see myself and others at stations all along the path that finally emptied into this merciless place, and in circumstances that at times I know to be wholly imagined, as when I see sometimes behind closed eyelids a dark landscape peopled with these small, tormented infants and mothers all scrabbling, as my grandmother ages ago scrabbled in the dirt, towards a vast, open grave. While chickens squawk and pluck and dance.

They are all jumping in.

Sarah Abernathy, I shall note, had become an old woman, susceptible to her own entrancements, by the time this criminal stain on her husband's character occurred to her. She had to become old, and wish these daughters were alive to rescue her from these walls, before she saw the pattern. I would come upon her, listless between her wheels, and say to her, "Sarah, where were you just then?" She would say, "I was daydreaming, I suppose. I was imagining one of my daughters had escaped. She was on her way here, in a red, open car, hair streaming in the wind. Coming to take me away from here."

At my insistence, and to the vast annoyance of those who manage this place, she had the police summoned, and she spelled his crimes out for them. If they looked in her family Bible, she said, they would find the precise dates for these homicides. If they looked in the yard at their old house, they would likely find the graves, shallow ones at that, since her husband was not one who hankered after heavy labor. Or he might have burned them, Sarah Abernathy said. He was always burning things, she said. As her time came close, she said, he would get his inferno going. At first his fires were huge blazes spread over open ground. Later he employed large oil drums into which he pitched her bloody sheets and over which he sprinkled gasoline. More than once she had stumbled from her bed to watch from her window her husband's busy silhouette against these leaping flames.

"Where is my child?"

"Dead. Go back to sleep now."

Afterwards he would crawl in beside her, smelling of smoke and gasoline.

"Don't cry," he'd say. "God is good."

Yes, it could very well be that he had burned away all the evidence. But they might find her children's bones. They might find some of her children buried in the yard.

The police said, What do you want us to do? As we understand it, they said, your husband is now dead. And the house you mention, well, that is long gone.

But Sarah Abernathy did not see that this made any difference. She wanted the record set straight. For history, she said. She wanted it officially recorded that she had brought these children in the world with nothing at all wrong with them.

The police took no action. Naturally, they did nothing. But the needless death of her children, who, if alive, would come and rescue her from this place, was all, or nearly all, Sarah Abernathy could talk about. And her talk raised a good deal of dust, of suspicion, and gave rise to other reports, because she was by no means the only woman in this place consumed by this issue.

We all wanted sons and daughters, husbands or lovers, to rescue us from this place. If we had none, we invented them.

Others here had stories similar to Sarah's. Many had scraps of paper, photographs, in their possession, rousted from old trunks filled with lace and linen, with bric-a-brac, with ancient dresses and pinafores, with wiry girdles and corsets and stays that no one wanted. They came to the meetings I and Sarah convened, clutching these scraps. They sounded out visitors, older relatives and friends not yet infirm. They had these people scouring the countryside, digging in old family cupboards and closets, chasing down the truth on these unexplained deaths.

On those gone missing, over the years.

They were alive. That was the hope. Some of these sons and daughters had survived the murderer's hand, and they would come. They would remove us to a better place. Wheel us into a less desolate world.

One woman, a Miss Rule, past one hundred and the oldest person ensconced here, swore before us all that *her* baby, the one baby she had brought into the world, had been fed to the dogs. Her father, up in the hills where they lived, had done this to her. He had fathered the baby, she said, and had then fed it to his dogs. Like Sarah Abernathy, she wanted him charged. She wanted matters set right. For history, she said. She had a younger sister, still alive, who could substantiate her every claim.

But the police, on this occasion, did not appear. They laughed, as Sarah Abernathy related this transgression to them. "You old folks watch too much TV," they said. "You ladies got too much mayhem on your minds."

Too much time, they said, on our hands.

After repeated calls, they agreed to have someone on staff here take down her statement, type it, and drop it in the mail. But no one did, and Miss Rule's health quickly worsened. We saw less and less of Miss Rule. Scant months later this enfeebled, incontinent woman died. She was found with a pillow over her face, her arms folded across the pillow, but it was agreed that she did not know what she was doing, if indeed she somehow accomplished this deed alone. If, indeed, she did not have help, or if one of our keepers, as Sarah Abernathy maintained, did not slip into her room in the dead of night and press the pillow over her face. Miss Rule was asthmatic. She was dying anyway. It did not take much.

She was a difficult woman, her facilities rarely intact. But she was exceedingly lucid when recounting her father's acts.

"Spit it out," Sarah had told her. "Cough it up."

Others among us began speaking out. Letters were being composed on every side. Most who could scribble were scribbling away. We would gather nightly, as though infected by a common disease, and read aloud these missives. Many began, "I want to recount here certain suspicions, or facts, about a death, or deaths, in my family, which I have never before revealed to anyone" – as that was the approved model.

This was, of course, before they confiscated our pens and paper, our notebooks and ledgers, and placed restrictions on our use of the common phones. In fact, these were removed, and subsequently, if calls were to be made, we had to beg use of the office instrument. There, someone was always standing by, listening, and often Sarah Abernathy, as happened with others countless times, had the phone snatched from her hand. The "lights out" hour was moved ahead by one hour. Then by another hour. Visiting hours were curtailed. Privileges eliminated. Vital care postponed. It was suggested, on more days than one, that we should confine ourselves to our rooms. New medicines were administered, initially to us individually, and later in our common food. The turnover in the staff was significant. The warm-hearted few, in whom we could confide, were replaced. The very air we breathed, over time, became a tainted air.

The north wing finally was sealed.

Sarah Abernathy was locked up naked in an empty room, and forced to stay there until she recanted.

"Look," they said to me. "Look what your sniveling inventions about the past have done." And they wheeled me to her door and bodily lifted me, compelling me to look through the small window at her in her nakedness in the white, empty room. They made others look as well, and what we all saw was Sarah Abernathy, skin and bones, with hardly any hair, cowering on the tiles. Cowering, or scrabbling, as my grandmother had done, on her stomach towards the door.

"There," they said. "See what your talk has come to?"

The truth is, these days, I have little strength for the enterprise. No doubt our fixations on this issue did carry us somewhat afield.

My memory dredges up ghosts from the past and I find I have little stamina for the naming of how they have passed from this world, or even if they have. And I see myself in large part as I see them. As some misty, unformed creature brought to an undefined precipice deep within the earth's core, with only a dim perception of how I have got where I am.

Yesterday – was it yesterday? – I was one minute at my window, looking out over the cornfield, struck by the sight of my mother's pretty legs lit by the sun, and the next minute I was riding with my slaughtered daughter in an open car. Her hair, and mine, were flowing in the wind. "Where are you taking me?" I asked, but whatever her answer was, or might have been, that same wind snatched it away. We were out on a country road, moving at dangerous speed. The fields were pretty, as I noticed from time to time, but mostly countryside is not what I saw. I saw split-rail fences, and a blur of fence posts, and an array of silent witnesses, upright and unsmiling, lining our path. "Oh, there are our dead," I said – "There you are!" – but my daughter did not take her eyes off the road or loosen her grip on the wheel.

The dead streamed by, but after a time I was scarcely aware of them. This place that had so long confined me was far behind now, and our car was hurtling with all dispatch to some final reckoning, or special dispensation, further along the road.

It was a March day, windy and cold.

– Interview with Ms. Gracie Hedgepeth, born 1899, recorded November 17, 1991, at Eagles Landing Rest Home.